Classic Sword & Sorcery

It was the magnificent Barbarian's most dangerous quest—to stop the wizard killer.

KOTHAR
and the
WIZARD
SLAYER

Book 5

by Gardner Francis Fox

Originally printed in 1970

digitally transcribed by Kurt Brugel 2017
for the Gardner Francis Fox Library LLC

Gardner Francis Fox (1911 to 1986) was a wordsmith. He originally was schooled as a lawyer. Rerouted by the depression, he joined the comic book industry in 1937. Writing and creating for the soon to be *DC comics.* Mr. Fox set out to create such iconic characters as the *Flash* and *Hawkman.* He is also known for inventing *Batman's* utility belt and the multi-verse concept.

At the same time, he was writing for comic books, he also contributed heavily to the paperback novel industry. Writing in all of the genres; westerns, historical romance, sword and sorcery, intergalactic adventures, even erotica.

The Gardner Francis Fox library is proud to be digitally transferring over 150 of Mr. Fox's paperback novels. We are proud to present - - -

Table of Contents:

Chapter One

Where the sea-waters lapped the rocky shore of Norgundy, a tall man wandered. He was clad in black cloak and nether garments that swayed with the breezes coming off the Outer Sea in a strange, writhing fashion, as though these garments might be alive. His step was firm, his eyes bright, as Luthanimor the Obsessed searched the sea-strand for those purplish shells that gave him the power to summon up the demons of the deep.

A great magician was Luthanimor, one versed in the spells and cantraips of his world. But he was fearful, for odd tales had come to his ears of late concerning the deaths of other necromancers, men as great or even greater than he when it came to dooming a man or a maid to the seven hells of Eldrak or summoning up the cacademons to destroy a warrior or a castle.

"Hastarth, send that I may find them," he whispered.

His head bent low as his eyes scanned the seashore where the ocean waters ran, frothing and bubbling before they sank down into the sand or ran out upon the wide shelf of beach sands. With but a few of the purple shells called myradex, he might summon up Omorphon, who would tell him how to protect himself against assassins.

Luthanimor did not see the thing that followed him crawling between the rocks, nor the long dagger it clutched in a rotting hand. Ever and always the lich watched the tall mage; ever and always it slithered closer, closer, making no sound on the rocks and on the stretches of sand. When the necromancer bent low above the shingle, the dead thing that followed him with the knife came to its height and ran, on decaying feet that made no sound, across the sand.

The dagger went deep between the mage's ribs. It was withdrawn, yanked back, and driven deep a second time. Luthanimor stiffened, his mouth opened as his bulging eyes stared sightlessly on the gray sky.

He slumped and fell, to lie lifeless.

In great Romm, in a cobble-stoned alleyway of that metropolis, Nebboth the warlock walked in the sidling gait that earned him the name of Crab among his fellows. A thin man with graying hair growing on a huge skull above a wry neck, he was forever shivering from cold except on the hottest days. He wore a black cloak and a hood up about his head, to shut off the cool winds sweeping across this poorer corner of the city.

Nebboth rarely came to the slums, he had servants to perform such menial tasks for him. But this night, he was seeking something special, two small girl children, sworn virgins, whom he would sacrifice to dread Eldrak in return for certain favors. Nebboth did not trust his hirelings; the children might be virginal no longer if he were to send huge Damthos after then. He would go himself, the lusts of the flesh no longer troubled him.

He was used to the sight of ragged men, of beggars and thieves who stalked these narrow byways for what they might beg or steal from honest folk. His sharp eyes darted into dark corners and recessed doorways, but he did not heed the tall, thin corpse in the torn burial robes, whose hand held a thin rope entwined about it.

Only when the mage stepped into a doorway set deep in a stone wall did the carrion thing move forward, snapping its right hand so as to free the thin cord. It whipped the cord in the air as the mage stepped into the doorway, thrust the door open. Before Nebboth could make a move, it wrapped the cord about his neck.

Its bony hands drew the cord tight while Nebboth clawed at the thing that was digging into his neck flesh, stifling him, cutting the air from his windpipe. Blue in his face was Nebboth, and the contortions of his lips and the flaring of his nostrils told of his agony.

For a few more seconds, life remained in the necromancer. Then he gave a great shudder and went limp. The lich released its hold, gathered up the thin cord, and rewound it about its hand.

It opened the street door, peered left and right, then broke into a lurching run along the cobbles.

One by one, all over Yarth from the flat-lands of Zoardar in the northwest to Zoane in Sybaros on the Outer Sea, from the snowy peaks of the Sysyphean Hills to the pyramids of Pshorm, the magicians of this world were meeting death. A bloody dagger, a worn length of killing cord, a sword or an ax, the weapon varied though the deed did not.

Anthalam in Wandacia, grim old Vardone of Ifrikon, many were the mages who went to join their ancestors in these early days of the Month of the Dragon. Fear was a blight among them, for the deaths that came to them tiptoed on unseen feet, hung poised on seemingly invisible daggers, for no man saw the coming of his death, always it was out of the shadows or the darkness.

In a tomb that housed the dead body of Kalikalides the magician, lay a sleeping woman whose long red hair fell over her white shoulders and down the stone walls of the ancient tomb, where her body rested atop the bier slab. She turned and twisted in her sleep. Uneasy was that necromantic slumber; her eyelids quivered, and the scarlet fans that were her lashes threatened to open at any moment. Her red lips moved, parting, and she uttered wordless little cries of dread and alarm.

In her dreams, Red Lori stood before the great stone throne where sat the dead mage whose tomb she shared. Kalikalides brooded down on her, but he shook his head and his lips quirked in what was meant to be a smile.

"My help cannot undo what has been done, Lori."

"It can prevent—more deaths Lord Kalikalides, have pity on them all. Your friends, your fellows, Luthanimor, Nebboth, Anthalam! All of them dead—slain by wizardry. A wizardry that comes from whence—no man knows.

"Soon all will be dead, all!"

"Except him who sends the slayers!"

"Ahhh—and who is it?"

In her dream she leaned closer, breathing harshly. The dead mage drummed fingertips on the broad stone arm of his stone throne in these charnel regions, making a faint, rhythmic sound even as he frowned.

"I do not know. He has covered his steps well, whoever he is. He has put a wall of demons about his deeds which even my eyes cannot penetrate."

"Then let me go, release me from the silver barrier Kothar placed upon your tomb door!"

A savage fury shook her as Red Lori spoke. Hate for the barbarian from the far Northlands, the blond sell-sword who had placed her here and sealed the edges of the tomb with molten silver, ate inside her. Before that, he had brought her captive over his shoulder out of the dark tower where she worked her incantations to aid Lord Markoth against Queen Elfa of Commoral, and had given her over to a silver cage hung high in the audience hall of the queen.

Kothar himself had freed her of the silver cage when she caused a she-demon named Ahrima to bring him to Commoral, but his barbaric wits had succeeded in imprisoning her once again, this time in Kalikalides' dank tomb.

"Free me," she whispered to the lich of the dead magician. "Free me, so I may help those of our wizard brotherhood left alive."

Kalikalides pondered, chin on fist. He sighed and in her dreams began to speak in his sepulchral voice. "Indeed, I like it no better than you, fair Lori. Magicians and warlocks should be sacred folk, freed from fear of the assassin's knife. But what may I do? I am long dead, as well you know."

"You know ancient spells. There must be one that will pass my body through the silver barrier."

"None! There are none." Red Lori sank weeping in stark rage to the stone floor, her hair like a scarlet mist about her body. Angrily she beat her white fists against the flaggings.

"Cursed be the name of Kothar! May his bones rot in his flesh and may his flesh stink with the suppurations of ulcerated wounds! May Omorphon sink his serpentine fangs in his liver and never let him go. May—"

"Hush, woman! Your eternal babbling disturbs my thought—and I am even now recalling an old spell, an incantation long forgotten by me..."

"Will it pass through silver?"

"Not your body, but a part of you. A spirit body that will appear to men in all respects as if it were real flesh and blood."

Excitement made Red Lori tremble. "It is enough," she breathed. "I know a way to join flesh body to spirit body All I ask is to go out of this place into the world—where Kothar lives!"

"You must forget vengeance for a while!" warned the magician, leaning forward on the stone throne from which he ruled the world his magic made before he died. "Were Kothar to suspect, he could blast your spirit self merely by touching you with that same silver which keeps you penned in here with me! Avoid angering him, Lori—if you would live and be free."

Between grating teeth she snarled, "I will be like a pulling maiden. I will serve him like a doting slave-girl. I will even—faugh!—make love to his barbarian body if it will help me."

"Pleasantly, Lori—pleasantly!"

She made herself smile. The smile transformed her lovely features, that had been contorted with rage and shame, into those of a young girl. Young was Red Lori when she smiled, like a shepherdess or a milkmaid in the meadow. Her mouth was a scarlet fruit sweetly curved and ripe for kisses, her red tresses like a shimmering veil hiding the white flesh of her shoulders and upper arms.

"See you do, witch-woman. The barbarian is no fool. If you intend to go to him—"

"Oh, I do—since I have a need for his sword and his muscles. Aye, I shall be the virginal innocent—until he gives me what I need to set myself free in truth."

"So be it. Then listen, this is what you must do."

Her slumber was troubled now, and she frowned, tossing slightly so that the worn velvet wrapping that covered her against the chill of the tomb slid down to reveal her ripely curving body clad in the Mongrol blouse and leather skirt which she had worn when she stepped into this tomb. Words came from her lips in broken phrases, at the sound of which the air grew cold and gelid in the stone sarcophagus. Faster she spoke and faster, committing those dread sounds to memory.

The cold woke her.

Red Lori sat up, clutching the velvet wrapping tighter about her shoulders. On the painted ceiling and walls of the crypt she could see the glittering hoarfrost and the hanging icicles which told her that her dream had been a reality of sorts. Her spirit had left her body, had gone into that charnel world of Kalikalides' own creation, where she had spoken with him.

Under her breath she whispered those words, shivering to the intense cold they summoned up. Now she knew that it had been no true dream but a journeying of her spirit into another realm. Kalikalides had placed a key in her white palms, a key which she would turn with words, to transport a part of her into the outer world.

Lying back, throwing aside the wrapping, she stretched out upon the top of the stone bier which held the rotting remains of the dead sorcerer. She understood now the reason for the cold, it was to hold her flesh in eternal ice while her ka went searching for the barbarian. Without its spirit, the flesh might putrefy; the cold would prevent this, would keep her body as it was now, while her spirit was still inside it.

"Great Thissikiss, lord of ice, of snow, of cold that numbs the soul! Hear my plea! Come unto me, come across the abysses and the voids of space and time that separate us! Take into your icy paws my body, shelter it from evil. And so benumb my every sense that my spirit may go forth, free of this fleshy trapping.

"Thissikiss, hear me!"

"I call you by Titicomti and by Alchollos, by Belthamquar the demon-father, and his dread mate, Thelonia!

"Come to me, Thissikiss. Come! Come! Come!"

From far away she seemed to hear the rumble of ice floes one upon another, caught the moan of the icy blast of wind that ranges the snow-clad hills and dales of fabled Hyperborea. A frozen breeze swept the chamber, and where it touched, the hoarfrost lay in thick white sheets. Her own body was beyond sensation, she realized. She felt neither heat nor cold nor did any odor touch her nostrils.

She was frozen flesh. Aye, frozen solid by Thissikiss, yet still alive!

For her spirit self could move, and rose and walk about this chamber, though her body was naked, with only the long red hair to hide her blue-veined flesh. She stood in the mausoleum and threw back her head and let soft laughter rise from her lips toward the icicled ceiling.

Free! At long last—free!"

"My thanks, Thissikiss. Keep me safe within your paws."

She mounted the stone steps leading upward from this subterranean vault to the upper level and moved toward the great stone slab that was the tomb door. Around this stone Kothar had placed the molten silver, sealing it, past which she could not go. Yet now she knew the way to travel beyond that barrier, in this shape that had substance and outline of a sort, though her true flesh and blood body lay frozen like unto death on the bier slab.

Red Lori lifted her hands and bent her head, placing her lovely features within her cupped palms, the better to concentrate her thoughts. She must make no error, without flaw must she speak the cantraipal formula that would permit her to slip from this tomb into—that other place where she would go.

She began to chant those words softly, almost to herself.

And the world around her reeled.

Chapter Two

The sun beat down with fury upon the golden sands of the desert which ran from the great rock scarps of the Haunted Regions as far eastward as the vast meadow-lands of Sybaros, and which, some men said, once had been an inland sea-bottom. On that vast sand sea, a horse and its rider moved slowly, steadily southward toward a range of low hills marking the southern boundary of this vast wasteland.

The rider was a huge man in mail shirt and with thick, sun-browned thighs showing between a plain leather war-kilt and tan leather war-boots. The muscles rolled in his arms and his long blond hair was caught in a leather thong knotted to keep the hair from getting in his eyes, for the wind whipped across these sandy wastes in a steady blow.

Beneath him the big gray warhorse moved with steady gait, walking leisurely in the heat, with a faint jingle of ring-bits and harness brasses. A sword with a red gem in its hilt, long in the blade and with a gently curving cross-hilt, gathered sunbeams to it and reflected them.

There were reflections of that same strong sunlight off metallic surfaces in the distance, where the rocks made a jagged carpet around a thin ribbon of road. Kothar the barbarian had seen those dancing motes of sunlight hours before; he had frowned suspiciously and watched them with hard blue eyes. His warrior instincts told him those bits of unusual brightness must be made by spear points and helmets where a body of men lay hidden among the crags.

Did any but himself know why he rode this way, southeastward through the desert sands and toward the rocky pass leading into Tharia? He had kept the secret to himself, trusting no man.

And yet—those bright sparkles amid the rocks spoke to him of an ambush in which he was to play the part of victim. He growled low in his throat, loosed the blade in its ornate scabbard, and shifted so that he might bring the quiver of arrows hanging behind him within easier hand-reach. The great horn bow, which had been a gift of the merchant Pahk Mah when he had rescued his daughter Mahla from the ensorcelments of Red Lori, was unstrung but close to his left thigh.

He rode on, alert and waiting. Where the sand made an upward slope before merging with the rock-land of the Tharian Pass, he drew rein and reached for a water-skin hung from the saddle pommel. He yanked the cork, tilted the bag to his lips.

"Half a mile ahead, Greyling, that's where they wait."

His mouth twisted into a wry grin. An itch was in his palm to hold his sword Frostfire against his enemies, he had been peaceful too long in Zoane and Atlakka, those cities of Sybaros where he had first learned of the ancient grave of Kandakore. Apparently others had heard of the grave and of his search for it.

Kothar lifted the horn bow into his hand, strung it with muscles bulging in his long arms—for the horn was tough and bent not easily—so that he might set the catgut string in place. Bow in his big left hand, he toed Greyling to a canter.

The hidden men planned to surprise him, but the barbarian swordsman would furnish the surprise. At least, this was his plan. But as he rode forward, he soon heard the ring of weapons clashing ahead of him and the shouts of warring men.

"By Dwalka, they've marked another for the slaying!"

His laughter boomed out and now the warhorse went at the gallop along the abandoned roadbed, for few travelers moved along this highway that had been built when Kandakore had ruled in long-forgotten Phyrmyra. From the hide quiver he drew out a long war-arrow and fitted it to the bowstring.

The clash of ringing swords was close, now. As Kothar rounded the bend in the old highway, he saw one man fighting off a dozen, a slender youth in mail and helmet, with a broken sword in his hand. He was dismounted and moving backward toward a high stone boulder where he could make a stand.

Kothar bent his bow, let loose the arrow. Straight it flew to bury itself in the chest of a burly man with a black beard. Again he fired, and now a lean man dropped. The grass grew thinner about the lone youth who fought so bravely with The broken sword. Some of his attackers turned toward the giant in the mail shirt galloping down on them.

The barbarian fired two more arrows, saw two more men drop. Then he was casting the bow aside, drawing Frostfire. The long blade lifted as he reined the gray horse to the side of the road and sent him thundering past three of the men who leaped for him.

A shearing swing of the steel and one man fell headless. Past a second bandit he drove the stallion, and this time the point stabbed into a throat just under a mail apron hanging from a helmet.

The galloping horse was past the melee now, turning to the hand on the worn leather reins. Kothar saw that the young man had thrown aside his broken sword, had snatched up another blade from the fingers of a dead man and was leaping forward on the attack.

The bandits did not wait to stand before these swordsmen. They scattered, running in among the rocks, slipping and sliding a path across them until they disappeared in the distance. Kothar reined up Greyling, let the horse snort and dance until its battle fever cooled. The youth before him stared up at the rider in the mail shift and grinned.

"My thanks, warrior. It was touch and go for a while there, after I broke my blade on a helmet."

Kothar stared down at a slim young man whose face was split with a reckless smile, whose long brown hair hung to his shoulders. He wore a mail shirt, a sword-belt about his middle. His red leather boots were dusty and split, here and there, by long usage. On the far side of the road was a sack he had dropped when the bandits came charging from the rocks.

"The name is Flarion," the youth informed him, bending to cleanse his bloody steel on the cloak of a fallen cut-purse.

"You don't look rich to me," the barbarian rumbled, dismounting to wipe his own blade dry. "So why should those bandits have attacked you? Unless you have stolen jewels in your sack or hidden on your person."

"Not I! lost all I owned in a game of dice in a Grandthal tavern. Now I'm just a wanderer. Like yourself." His grin showed fine teeth in a nut-brown face.

Kothar scowled. "They must have been after something."

"Oh, they were, they were. My life. I—er—angered a fat merchant by making love to his pretty wife before I knew that the merchant was not on caravan but merely in his counting house, and soon due home."

His laughter rang out, carefree and careless. "By Salara of the bare breasts! She was a woman, that one. Ignored by her fat husband. Too bad he interrupted us. I was about to make her disclose the hiding place of her jewels.

could have used the coins they'd fetch in a shop I know."

The brown head tilted sideways. "And you? No man rides this old road any more, unless he's running from an angry husband of King Midor's soldiery."

Kothar chuckled. "Or bound into Tharia to the haunted ruins of Phyrmyra, where Kandakore is said to have ordered his burial ten thousand years ago."

Flarion gaped, jaw dropping.

"The lost tomb of Kandakore! Is that your goal?"

"I'm tired of an empty belly, of a purse that's so lean all it holds is air. It's been a month since my throat tasted ale, or anything but a slab or two of dry bread and drier cheese. Gods, for a bit of meat and mayhap even a beaker of wine! The sell-sword business is poor, these days."

Flarion muttered, "They say his tomb is haunted."

"Aye, by ghouls and goblins, or worse." Brown eyes glinted through narrowed lids. "The old tales don't bother you? You'd risk being drained of blood or eaten in some dusty mausoleum?"

"If I could get a handful of gems or golden coins, it would be worth the risk."

He did not add that Afgorkon the Ancient had given him the choice of owning the sword Frostfire and little else; and that since he bore the sword, he had never been able to own more than a few silver deniers to rub together in his purse. Afgorkon had lived, a most potent sorcerer and wizard, more than fifty thousand years ago. His spirit still existed in a world of his own magical creation, across the abysses of astral Space.

His curse was as strong today as the big barbarian over whom it hung, however. So Kothar carried Frostfire while poverty was an ache in his empty belly. He paused now, letting go the edge of the dusty cloak that had served to clean his blade.

"And you? Where are you bound?"

Flarion shrugged. "Anywhere. I have no goal, except to find a wench to kiss and a pallet to bed her on after washing the dusts from my throat with a panniker of Tharian ale. If you want company, I'm your man. If you'll dare ghouls and hob-gobs, so will I."

"If the old stories are true; the tomb of Kandakore holds much treasure, more than enough to make two men rich beyond their dreams."

"Kandakore hid his tomb well, the tales say."

"Where treasure is hidden, there are maps to show its hiding place."

Flarion Snorted. "Aye, I know maps like that."

"But not—like this."

The barbarian reached into his leather belt-wallet, drew out a folded bit of parchment, tossed it across to the waiting youth. Flarion caught it deftly, opened it, his fingertips running over the smooth surface.

His eyebrows arched. "Sheepskin?"

"Human skin, or I miss my guess."

"Gods, maybe there is something to the old tales, after all. I suppose you've heard them, that Kandakore empowered Ebboxor, who was his mage to build his tomb well and hide it, then mark its location on the skin of his favorite slave-girl."

"I've heard rumors and legends."

Flarion knelt in the dust and spread the map on the road. "I wonder ... if this be the skin of that girl, then perhaps . . ." His fingertip scratched at a thin black line that showed where a road had been, long ago. "Dried blood, treated in some manner . . . by Ebboxor? It might be. And if this really is human skin, and I think as you do that it is, then . . . ."

His grin was broad. "Then by Salara's creamy bosom, I think you've got hold of something. How'd you come by it?"

"In Makkadonia where I was serving as sergeant of guards, following a little adventure of mine with Queen Stefanya of Phalkar, whereby I set her on her throne. It seems that King Horthon of Makkadonia has a few hated enemies. Among them was a certain Jokathides, one of the richer merchant princes.

"Well, King Horthon sent a few of his chosen guardsmen to loot the cellars beneath Jokathides' vast town house, which is so big it's

15

practically a palace. At one time, his basements were part of the palace of the Sassanidon line, which ruled Makkadonia long ago.

"We looted it, all right, and helped ourselves into the bargain to a few treasures we felt Horthon wouldn't miss. But Horthon is no fool, he knows what poor wages he pays his warriors, so he had other warriors intercept us before we could leave the cellars with our loot. The men were searched, all their little trinkets were taken away from them."

Flarion laughed softly. "But—not you!" Kothar rumbled laughter. "Well, I admit I heard what was happening, so I started off into another corner of the tunnels so I could hide the few things I'd managed to take. I went into another part of that basement where we hadn't been, and from the dust on the place nobody else had been there since the Sassanids were, dust, I'd wager. A part of the wall was cracked, broken."

He had peered into the darkness beyond the crack, smelling the dankness of old age, the mustiness. His hand slipped, and he saw that the brick against which he leaned his weight was loose. A few moments later he had made a hole wide enough to squeeze through, and when he was inside the hidden chamber, he struck sparks from flint and steel, lighted his tinder, and held up his small lamps.

There were tumbled, chests and dusty coffers here and there, with bars of gold and silver making small mountains. Dust lay thick over everything, so that he choked and coughed and had to spit to clear his throat. He moved about the chamber, examining everything. On the metal clasp of a small coffer, he had found carved the name: Ebboxor.

A blow from his dagger pommel snapped the rusted lock. Opening the coffer, Kothar found the parchment inside it. One touch of his fingers and he had known that this was human skin. Spreading out the vellum, he saw there was a map scrolled on that smooth surface.

Kothar chuckled. "I hid the thing flat against my chest under my mail shirt. It was so thin, nobody among the royal guards suspected I carried anything there.

"Soon after, I found an excuse to give up my employment and set out for these rocky wastes, beyond which the tomb of Kandakore is hidden."

"If you were in the royal guard, why is your purse so empty?"

"I spend the coins I earn as fast as my fists can close about them. I can't gather treasure and keep it—Afgorkon the Ancient sees to that—and so I enjoy life when life is good. When it isn't, I cut new holes in my belt."

Flarion nodded, folding over the map and handing it back. "I know the feeling. But if you've a mind to share your luck in exchange for a sword to stand beside your own, Flarion's your man."

Kothar watched while the youthful mercenary picked up his traveling sack, tossed it over a shoulder. Kothar put a foot into his stirrup, swung up on his horse. From here, the ride to the fabled tomb of Kandakore was but a league, not too far for a man who had walked across the western desert of Sybaros, all the way from Grandthal.

Their way led through the rock country and down a long slope toward the ruins of ancient Phyrmyra. The grave he sought was in Phyrmyra, if his map were true. As they came to a crown in the road, by standing in his iron stirrups the barbarian could make out the few columns and the tumbled building stones that were all that was left of once-great Phyrmyra, faint in the distant haze of twilight.

"We'll camp and eat, first," he said to Flarion trudging beside him in the dust. "There's a fountain in the city that still gives water, travelers have told me."

"There's also a curse on Phyrmyra," grinned the youth, shifting his sack to the other shoulder. "Something about, a leech that sucks the blood from a man and leaves him to die in raving madness."

The barbarian snorted. "I never heard anything about a leech. The traders I've spoken with said only that there was an evil in the old city which made them happy to shake its dust from their boots. They didn't linger long."

'We'll have to linger if we want to find that grave."

The barbarian merely grunted.

The came along the road into the twilight of the day, when the setting sun was a red ball low in the west beyond the Misty Swamps and the lands of the baron lords, The jagged rocks were behind them, while before them was a great plain where stood lonely orthon trees and berry-bushes, which gave ripe fruit now as they had when Phyrmyra had swarmed with people. It was a quiet, dreaming kind of day, and Kothar found himself beset by memories of past encounters with demons such as Azthamur, Abathon and Belthamquar. Those dread beings from beyond the spatial gulfs had good reason to hate Kothar the barbarian; he wondered if one or all of them might come to him in Phyrmyra.

He moved his shoulders angrily, as if to rid himself of phantoms. His hand touched his sword hilt lightly, then fell away. The gibbering imps of his imagination would not let him go: Something waited for him in the ruined city, of this he was sure.

The city stood a mile eastward of the road which at one time, according to old legend, had run through its foreign market-square. Now the columns and fallen pediments of the ruins showed only where a palace or a temple had been, with smaller buildings around it. Kothar turned Greyling toward the dead city.

Beside him, Flarion stumbled. "Hells of Eldrak," he rasped. "What's this?" His toe kicked sand, showing part of a bone gleaming whitely in the dusk of evening. Flarion spat. "A dead man, his skeleton."

There were other skeletons, the barbarian saw, shifting his glance downward and along the sands where his companion walked. Whitened bones, bits of rib-cases, a hip bone, ulnar and tibia here and there made a trail out of Phyrmyra toward the road.

"They can't hurt us," he snarled. Flarion laughed softly. "What made them bones—can! Still, for a treasure, a man must take risks."

They came among the standing columns and the fallen stone lintels in the first night darkness, with the stars glittering overhead and a wind moaning off the plain. "A dismal place," thought the barbarian, glancing around him as he came down out of the kak, "and if it were not for the map and the tomb it shows, I'd bed down on the clean dirt beside the highway."

He tossed a food bag to Flarion, with a wine-skin. He unsaddled Greyling, rubbed him down, fed him oats in a leather pouch. The tinkle of water caught his ears, he turned from the horse and moved along what had been a wide road once but was no more than blocks of stone, tilted and awry, between which the sands had settled.

The water was coming from a rock wall out of which a worn stone conduit jutted. The water was probably forced upward from pressures below the ground, he told himself. He was about to sip when a voice breathed words into his ears.

18

"No, barbarian!" Kothar jerked erect, hand on his dagger pommel.

"Who spoke?" he growled. Soft laughter mocked him, and the barbarian showed his teeth in a cold grin. "Red Lori! I'd know that laugh in the deeps of hell where it belongs."

"The water—slays, Kothar!"

He scowled at the conduit, at the crystal stream flowing from its length. He turned and glanced at Greyling and at Flarion, crouched before the fire which he had begun with dried twigs collected from below some orthon trees.

"You have water in your skins. Use that. Drink not this, on peril of your life."

He rubbed his blond head with his hand, scowling. He knew Red Lori well enough to understand that she considered him to be her own special property, to be executed and tortured in her own good time, to pay him back for the things he had done to her.

He knew also that she was still imprisoned in Kalikalides' tomb in Xythoron. Well, she had come to him at other times in his wanderings over the face of Yarth. Inside ale tankards, in the leaping red flames of his campfires, in dreams, he had seen her beautiful face and heard her words inside his head.

"You have seen the skeletons. Those belonged to men who came here parched with thirst and drank the waters of Phyrmyra. Be warned."

Kothar scowled, shrugged. He turned away, went back to the campfire, where Flarion was turning slabs of meat above the flames on a crude spit. "Ware the water. It's poisoned,' he muttered, reaching for his water-skin. "Now how would you know that?"

"I have a personal demon all my own. She helps me stay alive, from time to time. It is a whim of hers, because she hates me very much."

The mercenary considered this, squinting up at the giant on the other side of the fire. He nodded slowly. "If you say so."

They ate sitting on the ground, slowly and with relish, and drained more than half the contents of the wine-skin. Cold was in the air here, for with the passing of the sun the ground lost much of its heat, and the wind was off the sea to the west, tainted with salt and chill.

With a muttered word, Kothar reached for the fur wrap that served him as cloak and saddle blanket. He drew it about his huge body, lay down with his feet toward the fire. A moment more Flarion waited, then drew a worn military cloak from his own sack and lay back, eyes closed.

The fire crackled, popped. Kothar slept as does an animal, with only half his mind, his ears alive to the night sounds about him. Once during the night he rose from his fur wrapping and placed more twigs and branches on the fire. He stood a moment, staring about him at the distant rocks, the vast plain on which ancient Phyrmyra had rested. Then he slipped back into the fur wrapping.

He did not see the men who waited among the rocks and watched. They were crouched low with the rocks between them and the distant ruins. They could not be seen, but they watched the wink of red that was the campfire.

The morning sun was minutes old when the barbarian stirred and threw aside the big bearskin covering. He lay a moment, staring at the blue sky shot with red streamers. Then he was up and moving about the little camp, building up the fire, lifting, the spade and pick he had brought with him from Zoane.

The smell of roasting meat roused Flarion, who came to stretch and yawn beside the flames, then bent to mix flour from a sack and water from his skin container, placing the biscuits on flat rocks to bake. He took the map. Kothar handed him and spread it out on the ground so they might examine it while they ate.

"Here,” said Kothar as he munched, tapping the human skin with a forefinger, “is The Temple of Salara. You'll note that it's right beside the water fountain. Now eastward from the temple, five hundred paces, is the statue built to honor Kandakore.”

"And below the statue, his grave.”

We'll dig when we're done eating.”

Kothar swallowed a final sip of wine before tossing the skin to his companion and rising to his feet. In his big hands the spade and pick seemed almost tiny as he walked across the tumbled flagstones of this old city square toward the wind-eroded remnant of what had been a carving of the love goddess.

His eyes measured the distance between the statue and the flowing water of the stone pipe. Five hundred paces; he marked them off slowly, thoughtfully.

With his spade, he dug out dirt and sand until the base of what had been a statue of Kandakore was revealed. He labored for close to an hour until the sweat dripped from his face. Then Flarion came to spell him.

When the flagstones all around the statue were cleared, the mercenary leaned on the spade. "There's no opening in the flagstones," he pointed out, tapping them with the edge of the spade.

"I can see that for myself. It comes to my mind that the statue itself may hold a clue as to its opening."

"You mean, it could be lifted, to disclose a hole?"

"Something of the sort, yes." They strove until their muscles creaked, but the granite base could not be budged. Kothar Snarled and moved back, walking all around that stone weight. The sun was higher in the morning sky, it cast dark shadows beyond the base. Kothar studied those shadows a moment, frowning, running his eyes along the edges of the giant block.

There appeared to be a space between the statue and the flagstones, just the merest fraction of an inch. The barbarian knelt, let his eyes run there. He nodded, rose to his feet.

"The base doesn't set flat," he said. "It's raised above the flagstones. Now I wonder why."

"Could we put a metal bar under it? Wedge and lift?"

"No, no. Perhaps the statue swings."

They set hands to the warm stone base and thrust hard. Nothing happened. "The joinings may be rusted," Kothar growled, and heaved again.

They were rewarded by the faint rasp of old metal. At the same time, the block gave, slipped sideways. Flarion yelled encouragement. They dug their toes into the sand tranches between the flagstones of this square, and their muscles swelled.

Slowly, as rusted metal grated, the thing moved, ponderously, with a muffled clank of hidden machinery. And Kothar felt the pavement under his war-boots sink.

"Get back," he cried, pausing to stare downward.

21

A section of the paving-stones was tilted at an angle, forming a trapdoor. Dirt and sand ran down into the small opening before the stone base. Flarion moved to the other side of the block, put palms to its roughened surface.

"We can get better purchase here he called. Kothar nodded, stepped around to join him. Once begun, the further moving of the rock slab on its metal fulcrum was much easier. In moments it was swung completely sideways. The section of paving-stone had fallen downward, hung on stone hinges. As he came around to stare down into that dark abyss, he saw stone steps inset into a rock wall.

He swung down onto that ladder, began to descend into darkness. Flarion was on hands and knees, following his progress. "Do you have a lamp of some sort? A torch in your bags?"

"I was hoping to find a torch or two down here. There's a small oil lamp in my gear. Will you fetch it?"

Flarion ran, Snatched up a tiny brass lamp, touched flame to its wick. With the lamp in hand he went down the ladder until he stood on a stone floor beside the Cumberian.

"Gods of Thuum," breathed Flarion, staring. They stood inside a small chamber the walls of which were painted to represent scenes and incidents out of the life of the long-dead Kandakore. Here he stood with a foot upon the neck of an enemy bowed before him, there he sat his throne, receiving gifts from groups of travelers from foreign countries. A long marble table held jars and pots in which food had been sealed.

Beyond this dusty antechamber stood a door studded with brass fittings, proclaiming the fact that beyond the door was the burial tomb of Kandakore the Unconquered. For uncounted ages, this room had known not the footsteps of men, it had stood lost to the world, remote, part of the almost forgotten, fabulous realm of Phyrmyra.

Kothar shook his shoulders against his awe. He moved toward the door with Flarion at his heels, clasping the lamp. A touch of the hand pushed open that brass-hung doorway on its copper hinges.

Flarion lifted the lamp, held it high. "By Dwalka!" bellowed Kothar.

A woman sat on the bier, slab, knees together, hands folded in her lap. She wore the garments of a Mongrolian maiden, leather jerkin thonged to contain the fullness of her breasts, a short leather skirt, neat

22

leather sandals. Long red hair tumbled down over her shoulders. Her face, in the golden lamplight, was very lovely.

Chapter Three

The barbarian stood paralyzed with shock. "Red Lori!" he bellowed at last, in utter amazement.

"You know her?" Flarion wondered.

"Kothar," breathed Red Lori, "my darling" She came off the stone bier slab, ran to the Cumberian and flung her bare arms about his neck. Against his lips she pressed her mouth, then seemed to shrink from him.

"Forgive me!" she whispered. "I could not help it. I've been here so long—put here by a wizard's curse—alone in the dark. . . ."

"Poor girl," breathed Flarion. "Damned witch-woman," growled Kothar. Kothar fought the emotions inside his giant frame. That touch of soft lips to his, the momentary brush of female flesh and the clasp of bare arms about his neck angered him, because he liked that kiss, that embrace. And he knew Red Lori too well not to know that it must be part of an act. She wanted something of him.

Flarion reproved him. "How can you say such a thing, Kothar? She's been here because of a curse. And—she loves you."

"Oh, I do. I do!" Lori nodded, glancing from the younger man to Kothar. "I've always loved him, even when he was carrying me out of my dark tower in Commoral City to have me placed inside a silver cage."

There were tears in her eyes as her white hands wrung together. Her warm green eyes pleaded with the Cumberian. She took two steps toward him, let him feel the softness of her body, putting both arms about his middle and hugging him. Her perfumed red hair lay pillowed on his mailed chest.

"Now you have found me, Kothar. Take me with you, out of this place. I beg it of you. Do you want to see me on my knees?"

The grip of her arms loosed and she sank downward to kneel before him, face upturned, eyes wet, tears moving down her cheeks. Kothar stared down at her, knowing dully that he was lost. He could deny this woman nothing. There was an affinity between them. The Fates had made them enemies but the Fates could not control the wild thudding

24

of his heart at her kiss, nor still the male flames in his flesh that leaped at contact with her body.

"Here, now. Get up, Lori." His huge hands lifted her until she rested against him on tiptoes, her palms spread on his shoulders, her wet eyes smiling, echoed by the sweet curving of her lips. Slowly her hands crept upward as her bare arms lifted to clasp him about the neck.

"Darling Kothar," she breathed. The barbarian was of half a mind to turn her and whack her backside with a big palm, but it had been a longtime since a woman had pressed herself against him. He admitted grudgingly that he found it a pleasant thing. Her moist red mouth was close, slightly parted, as if begging for his kiss.

Kothar growled his helplessness against her allure. His arms tightened around her slim waist, his mouth closed on hers. He held her, swaying slightly, while Flarion stared at the ceiling of the tomb, at its painted walls, at the stone sarcophagus that held all that was left of King Kandakore.

Lori pushed away, flushing, lifting her hands to set to rights her long hair, smiling tenderly up at him, eyes shy and half hidden under her long lashes. She seemed like a maiden newly fallen in love. There was nothing of the arrogant witch-woman in her manner.

"What brought you here, Kothar?" she whispered.

"Treasure," answered Flarion. "But there's nothing here."

Red Lori pulled her green eyes away from Kothar's stare, turning to glance about the burial chamber. "This tomb is sacred to the death god. The royal treasures are kept in another place."

"Where?" asked Flarion. "Why do you know so much about the burial habits of the Phyrmyran kings?" wondered Kothar.

"The demon who put me here told me of them," said Red Lori hurriedly. "He—ah—taunted me with the fact that in the next room was enough gold and jewels to buy half a world, while I must remain here, shut in and starving."

"You can't have been here too long," rumbled Kothar, running his eyes up and down her curving body, so blatantly exposed in the scanty Mongrol garb.

Lori laughed at him, lifting her arms about her head and turning to let him see what he would of her shapeliness. "Not long, no. I have an

25

appetite for food, but I'm not starving."

Suspicion awoke in Kothar, who still did not trust this redheaded woman. She had vowed vengeance on him, she had hated him with a furious savagery; he did not believe she could have forgiven him so easily for locking her away with dead Kalikalides.

And yet—

Her bare legs shone in the lamplight under the short leather skirt, admirably rounded and enticing. Her hips swung with a wanton little wiggle, her body was all sweet curves and smooth white skin as she ran past the stone bier toward a farther wall. Her hands and fingers fumbled there until Flarion went with the brass lamp to show her the raised stonework she sought.

She turned a stone flower and part of the wall opened with a creak of unused hinges. Flarion cried out, pushing the lamp into the opening she had revealed.

"Kothar—look!" he cried.

Lori turned held out her arm to the big barbarian, clasping his fingers with her own warm hand, leading him through the opening.

They stood in a room as large as the burial chamber. Golden statues of men and women and beasts stood in orderly rows beside a painted boat in which the mummified body of a sailor sat with the helm in a dusty hand. Metal and wooden coffers lay upon long tables set flush to the walls.

The floor was unmarked, covered by a thin layer of dust. Flarion pointed at it, shouted, "No one's been in here since they closed the place. No grave robber has ever found this place. It all belongs to us. To us!"

He ran to a table, put down the lamp so he could lift the lid of the nearest coffer resting there. He gave a cry when the lid went back, The lamplight showed hundreds of round golden coins—dildaks, they were, the forgotten coinage of ancient Phyrmyra. Each one was worth a fortune because no other coins like them existed in the present world. And also tiny bars of that same precious metal placed side by side. Flarion dug his fingers into that treasure hoard, letting coins and bars sift between them.

Red Lori drew Kothar to another coffer, extending her hand and

26

raising the carved lid to show him red jewels and blue gems, precious diamonds and green emeralds. The ransom of ten emperors stood on this tabletop. Kothar growled his delight in what he saw, he lifted out a great ruby, held it to the lamplight. It glowed and sparkled as if with inner flames.

"It's too bad you cannot keep it," she whispered.

His eyes sparked. "Ah! You know about my curse?"

"You can keep no wealth but Frostfire, your sword, Oh, yes. I know all about Afgorkon and how he gave you the blade under a geis."

The barbarian lifted her hand and dropped the giant ruby into her palm. "Then you keep this, Lori. It matches your hair."

Her red-nailed fingers tightened on the jewel. Her glance at him was curious, enigmatical. "You would do that? Give me this ruby?"

"Why not? Help yourself." His hand waved around the room. He chuckled, "One of us might as well share these riches. You and Flarion take what you will. I'll content myself with a few coins here and there, enough to keep Greyling and myself in food and shelter."

Lori narrowed her eyes, tilting her head to one side as if to study him more closely. "There is a way, you know . . . by which the spell of Afgorkon may be removed."

He shook his head, snorting. "No man dares do that. Ulnar Themaquol told me as much, that time I solved the riddle of Pthoomol's labyrinth. Other mages have hinted the same thing, Kylwyrren of Urgal among the rest. There is no way for me to own anything but Frostfire."

"And I say there is, barbarian!"

A little of her old pride glared out at him as she straightened. She was a sorceress of no mean repute, he told himself. She had been the helpmate of Lord Markoth in that king's desperate fight against Elfa" of Commoral. She had almost bested Kazazael, who served the queen in that struggle.

"How may it be done?"

"Take you what you will, and then do what I shall say," she bade him, turning away to cross the chamber until she stood before the painted solar boat in which the embalmed sailor sat. She stood there, searching the boat, it seemed, for something which should be there.

Kothar shrugged, turned to the table. He said to Flarion, "Take only what you need. Gold and jewels weigh heavily on a walking man."

"I'd bring it all with me if I could. Gods! Saw you ever wealth like this? Kandakore must have been a happy man."

"Legend says he died loveless and hated by his people. No, Flarion, I don't think wealth alone makes a man happy."

The youthful mercenary grinned. "Then let me be unhappy, but loaded down with so much wealth one man could not spend it all in a long lifetime."

Kothar filled his leather belt-purse with gold coins and bars, and with a few of the larger jewels. Its sides bulged when he was done. He turned to look at Red Lori.

The girl was holding a golden scepter in which was set a magnificent diamond. Her fingertips caressed the carven length of the scepter, lingered over the huge gem. Her eyes lifted to stare at Kothar when she felt his look.

"With the help of his court wizard, Kandakore is said to have stolen this scepter from the demon Bathophet," she said softly. "It possesses strange powers. I choose it as my share." Her cheeks dimpled in a smile. "It may come in handy when I recite the spell to Bathophet which will free you from Afgorkon's curse."

The barbarian grunted. Deep in his heart he did not believe there was any such spell. Surely those master magicians, Ulnar Themaquol and Kylwyrren, would have known of it. But because he wanted to believe, because of the gold and jewels making such a satisfying weight at his belt, he nodded.

"Then keep it, and whatever else you see." She shook her head. "I choose you, Kothar, to be my share. And with you, your purse. That is one reason. why I am so anxious to cast my spells to Bathophet. Whatever is yours becomes mine, as it were."

She laughed softly, eyes glowing. The Cumberian felt like a slave selected for the buying. He had no way to sway the Fates, he must go where bidden by this red witch, do as she would have him do.

He felt a momentary anger at this loss of his male independence. But Red Lori came close and ran her soft fingertips across his lips, and the big barbarian shivered and stared deep into her green eyes, losing himself in their promise of delights to come.

Flarion said, "I can carry no more." They went up the stone ladder, Flarion leading the way and following him, the girl. Kothar mounted easily after them. They came out into the sunlight of high noon, with the air about them sweet with the fragrance of growing things. The sky seemed bluer, the day more lovely, because of the treasure each one carried.

Flarion came to join Kothar in his task of pushing the statue base back into place so the trapdoor would lift and lock. Now no wandering beggar would find the golden hoard which they considered their own.

Kothar said, "We stay the day, and hunt for food. We will sleep the night here, then travel in the morning. It is a long ride to Thoxon in Makkadonia."

"Why go to Thoxon?" Flarion said. "Better to cross Tharia and head toward Zoane," Lori nodded.

Kothar glanced at her. "Why Zoane?"

"Zoane is the largest city in Sybaros. There I can find what I'll need to prepare those spells to Bathophet for you. Zoane borders the sea, and it is in the sea that the lost tablets of Afgorkon are to be found."

Flarion laughed. "And Sybaros is a rich country. King Midor always seeks for soldiers to enlarge his army against attack by Makkadonia and Tharia. I have my sword to sell, so have you, Kothar."

The Cumberian shrugged. "It matters not to Kothar where Greyling walks. I'll get my bow, there must be a few hares in this wilderness to furnish our supper."

He went on foot out onto the plain bordering the ruins of Phyrmyra. The vast flatland harbored no shelter for the great stags and doe that abounded in the northern forests. Here were merely hares and other small game such as the toy-deer and the addabear. Kothar was a master hunter, he walked more softly than the wind, he could freeze and wait for his prey like a statue.

Between some low bushes he sighted two big leaper hares. They nibbled the succulent fruit and the stalks of a nearby berry-bush. They did not see him, and he was downwind of them. Carefully he placed an arrow to its string, sighted. He released the catgut string, saw the arrow soar and drop.

29

One of the hares toppled over, impaled on that long war-arrow. The second animal froze in surprise and terror for the instant that the barbarian needed to nock and release another shaft.

He came back into their little camp oddly proud, listening to Lori exclaim over his prowess with the horn bow. Flarion had found a little stream some distance away, had filled their skins with cool liquid. Enough flour was left in Kothar's saddle bags so that the girl could make small bread loaves.

They feasted together as the sun was setting. When darkness came, Kothar lifted his fur wrap and extended a hand toward Lori. She smiled faintly, let him help her to her feet, and walked with him into the darker shadows away from the fire where Flarion was curled up and ready for sleep.

"You share my fur," he growled, spreading it on the ground.

Her eyebrows rose. "As free woman?" He turned to stare up at her. "Of course. You're no slave."

"You saved me from Kandakore's tomb. It is the law of Yarth that when a man has saved a Woman's life, she belongs to him unless she purchases her freedom with a gift." Her green eyes mocked him.

"Have you a gift for me?" She shook her head, smiling. "I shall not give you the scepter which you said I could have. And that is all I own."

"Make a gift of your body," he told her softly. She smiled at him, head tilted to one side even as her white fingers began untying the thongs of her Mongrol jerkin. He could not read the emotion in her slanted green eyes but he had the uneasy feeling that she mocked him, though she said pleasantly enough, "Now that is a good idea, Kothar of Grondel fjord. I shall offer you my body."

The leather thongs were undone and her breasts pushed into the opening of the jerkin. He was faintly surprised to find them so full. Then she shoved down the garment and her leather kilt and her nakedness was a gleaming ivory loveliness in the darkness. Kothar sighed, not caring whether this woman taunted him or not; he had to have her flesh in his embrace.

She laughed and stepped to him, throwing her arms about his neck and letting him feel the moist warmth of her lips. They swayed a moment, clinging tightly, before the barbarian dragged her down onto

30

his bearskin cloak.

The fire winked and glowed in the night. The tip of a sword at his throat awoke the barbarian. He opened his eyes, but lay still. His slightest movement might drive that steel into his throat. Flarion? Was it Flarion who stood over him with a sword in his hand? Had the possession of the gold and jewels driven the youth to madness?

"Get up, you," said a harsh voice.

The sword-point went away. Beside him, a naked Lori would have clothed herself in the Mongrol garments, but a foot kicked them away and a man laughed. Kothar rose to his feet slowly, growling.

Flarion was standing beside the fire, scowling darkly. Five men— Kothar recognized them as the bandits whom he and Flarion had driven off in the Tharian Pass—stood grinning at them. Behind him, Red Lori was tugging at a corner of the bearskin cloak to hide her body.

"You've found treasure," muttered the man with a sword in his hand, grinning. He bounced the leather belt purse in his hand. As the Cumberian watched, he opened the bag, poured out a stream of gold coins and jewels onto the ground. "Where's the rest of it?"

Kothar shook his head. A scarred man snarled to one side and lifted out a dagger. "I know ways to make him talk."

"No, Fithrod, no violence—not yet, at least." One of the bandits approached the leader, the tall man with the pointed steel-helmet and chain mail which he had taken from one of the Southland caravans. He offered him the sack in which Flarion had put his own coins and jewels.

"A pretty haul," nodded the leader, watching his fellow bandit pour that treasure close to the small pile which had come from Kothar's belt purse. "Enough here to keep a dozen men in wealth the rest of their lives."

"Then take it and let us go," Flarion snarled. "Why should we do that when it appears you know the secret of old King Kandakore? Show us the treasure and I'll kill you swiftly, without pain."

Against his arm, the Cumberian could feel Red Lori shuddering. Before she had lost her witch-like powers, she would have made short work of these bandits. A few words, a gesture in the air, and a demon such as Asumu or Omorphon or even Belthamquar, who was the father of demons, might have come at her summons to swallow the thieves. He himself was unarmed Frostfire was thrust into the belt of the man in the pointed helmet. So was Flarion.

"Stake them out," the bandit chieftain snapped.

Two men threw Flarion to the ground, extended his arms and legs, A third man ran for wooden pegs, hammered them in with a rock. Leather thongs were attached to his spreadeagled arms and legs.

Kothar was quiet. Unarmed, he would be no match for the bandits. Yet he had no intention of lying down obediently while they tied him down for the sun to bake or to allow their knives to slice him into bloody gobbets. And so he waited, tensed, not betraying his mood. "The girl now," said their leader. And Kothar leaped. His left fist drove into the face of the bandit chieftain as his right hand closed about the jeweled hilt of Frostfire. With a savage yank he tore it free of the leather belt as blood spurted from the crushed nose his fist had struck. The blued steel came into the sunlight.

Kothar was moving before his sword was completely free of the belt, he was grasping Red Lori, swinging her off the ground and onto his hip as his sword's edge slashed downward across a bandit's shoulder. Instantly Frostfire was turning, parrying a blow from a scimitar, then thrusting deep into the belly of a third outlaw.

The clang of steel on steel was music in the ears of the giant barbarian. His martial spirit reveled in these sounds of combat, the harsh breathing of fighting men, the stamp of feet along the ground, the rasp of sword-blades where they met in mid-stroke. He parried effortlessly, seeming to handle two swords at once as his massive muscles rolled beneath his tanned hide. His keen eyes, trained to swift observation along the ice fields and forested hills of the northern lands from which he came, saw openings through which Frostfire darted like the tongue of an angry snake.

Back and forth between the ruins he surged with the redhead hanging onto him, gasping at times when the steel came close to her fair skin, eyes wide under long red lashes as her naked body felt the powerful play of his own. Her arms were clasped about his throat, yet not too tightly, as she sought to make herself less of a burden for him.

As he fought, the Cumberian drove the bandits away from the youth stretched on the ground between the pegs, fearing they might slay him

32

in an attempt to make Kothar surrender. His blade wove back and forth like the bobbin of a loom, stabbing, slashing, thrusting. Where he had been, lay the bodies of dead men, mute testimonials to the fury of his sword.

Against a marble pillar he cornered the bandit leader and the last of his men, and there he slew them with two savage swipes of his steel. A headless body leaned its shoulders against that column as a head went bounding off across the ground, gouting blood; Kothar drove Frostfire through the chest of the chieftain until its point grated against the marble behind it.

His left arm loosed its grip, Lori sank down onto her bare feet. "You fight with the fury of a desert storm, Kothar," she whispered, awed.

He grunted, "Go put some clothes on, girl before the sunburns your backside for you." His palm clouted a soft buttock, making her stumble.

Her laughter rang out as she whirled to face him, lifting her long red hair in her hands. "You and I—we could rule the world, if we wanted! You with your fighting ability, I with my necromantic wisdoms."

He eyed her dubiously, "If you still possess those powers, why didn't you use them?"

She shook her head. "I save them—for a greater need."

"What need?"

"I may not tell you—just yet." She scampered toward the sleeping fur and her leather jerkin and skirt. As she drew them on, she watched the barbarian kneel and slash the bindings that held Flarion.

They found food in the leather bags the bandits carried, and water in the skins attached to their belts. Kothar crammed one of the sacks full and tied it to Greyling's saddle. Into the kak he hoisted Red Lori when they were done eating, and turned his face eastward toward the Sea.

Flarion trudged beside him. "Where do we go?"

"To Zoane in Sybaros."

Zoane was the largest and richest of all the wealthy cities of rich Sybaros. It was a port city on the Outer Sea, its galleys and sailing ships plied those salt waters as far south as the Oasian jungles, as far north as Thuum, and to distant Isphahan in the east. Its taverns were floored with semiprecious stone tiles, its streets with slabs of marble.

33

Its palace and its smaller castles were breathtaking in their loveliness. No man who ever saw Zoane walked away without a touch of awe deep inside him.

Flarion shrugged. "Zoane or another, what does it matter? I'm a rich man, and I can spend my gold there as well as elsewhere. Still, prices are always high in Zoane."

From her perch in the saddle, Lori laughed. "Come with us, young Flarion—and be richer than you dream!"

He turned and grinned up at her. "What schemes are you plotting in that pretty redhead of yours?"

"I ride to find death—and slay it!"

Flarion gaped at her, thinking she jested.

Kothar merely scowled.

Chapter Four

The tavern was alive with sound in the smoking light of a thousand candles as the men at the wooden tables pounded on their tops with wood and leather ale-mugs. The slap of bare feet on wet wood, the tinkle of zither strings, the hoarse, shouts and the shrill laughter of drunken women wafted out into the marble streets of the city by the Outer Sea. Three travelers, each wrapped in long woolen cloaks against the mists of the water, paused at the door of the tavern, listening to the sounds, sniffing at the odors of roasting beef and cooking lamb.

Overhead swung a wooden sign carved to resemble a dolphin, painted black. The smallest of the three travelers waved a pale hand. "It is here, the Tavern of the Black Dolphin, that we are to meet him."

Kothar rumbled, "All this secrecy for a ship? I could steal you one with less trouble."

"It isn't any ordinary ship I need, Kothar."

The barbarian hunched his massive shoulders impatiently, went to stand at the partly opened door, looking into the seaside alehouse. His eyes saw the naked woman who danced on the tabletop, but he paid her no heed; his eyes were turned inward as if to search his own mind.

For more than a week they had been on the road to Zoane, joined together in good fellowship, with something more than fellowship between himself and the red-haired witch-woman. Yet now that they were in Zoane, Red Lori had fallen secretive, mysterious. She made plans without consulting him, without so much as a by-your-leave. He felt anger growing and was surprised to find that a faint jealousy lay inside him, as well. Oddly, he wanted the girl all to himself, he did not want to share her even with the plan she had in mind.

A soft hand touched his. He looked down, seeing her green eyes staring oddly at him. "I have my reasons, barbarian," she whispered. "Bear with me for a little while."

He shrugged and stood aside so that she might walk ahead of him into the tavern. Flarion came after them, treading lightly, staring with bright eyes at the belly-dancer who flaunted her flesh in the candlelight, stamping and pivoting on the tabletop.

Red Lori chose a table close to the wall, where her gaze could scan the faces of the roisterers. Kothar sat to her right, Flarion slipped onto the bench to her left. A serving maid ran to greet them, tray and wiping cloth in her hands.

"Ale," rasped the Cumberian, "and wine for the woman. And don't forget the food platters."

Flarion said, "Fetch the ale in large tankards. We've thirst enough to empty an ocean, girl. And who's that dancing so excitingly?"

"Cybala," Smiled the girl and turned to go. Red Lori chuckled as she saw the eager interest of the youth. "Go talk to her, Flarion. Offer her gold, you will—but bring her to the table."

In surprise, the mercenary glanced at the redhead. "Bring her here? But why?"

"We have a need for her." Flarion scowled. "I can understand why I might have need for her, having been traveling companion to you two lovers all the way from Phyrmyra, but why you have a wish for her company is beyond me."

"It will be clear, in time. Just fetch her." The girl on the tabletop paused, arms up flung and head thrown back, her ripely curved body quivering. She was olive skinned and with long black hair, and though she was younger even than Flarion, there was an eternal wisdom in her black eyes and in the languishing smile on her red mouth. She posed, letting the shouts and the applause roll around her. Then she bent, lifted the thin wrap that she had tossed aside when mounting the table and threw it about her nudity.

Hands reached for her, voices called. She ignored them to step down onto a chair and to the rush-strewn floor. She moved through the voices and the hands, and marched toward a narrow, curtain-hung doorway on the far side of the big common room.

Suddenly, a slim mercenary in worn leather and mail shirt was before her, eyes worshipful. She paused, frowned, went to turn aside.

"She would speak to you," said Flarion, pointing.

"She?" In surprise Cybala halted, eyebrows lifting. With female curiosity, she turned, stared where the youth gestured.

Across the room, black eyes touched green and-were held. As the snake holds the hen, she went rigid, feeling her senses slip away from her. "Come to me," the eyes said. "You have no will, Cybala the tavern dancer. So—come to me." And with a sigh that was half a sob, Cybala let the mercenary clasp her hand and draw her along with him through the throng.

"We would make you rich, Cybala," said Lori softly when the girl was beside her on the bench.

"And in return for such wealth?"

"We have a need for you." The green eyes still held her in thrall, the dancer found. There was a strange languor in her flesh born not of the physical world but of the mind. Almost against her will, she asked, "But what may I do for—such as you?"

"You will learn—in time. What will it cost to buy your bondage from the tavern owner?"

"He took me in when I was starving, and fed me. I could always dance, I was taught by slave owners from Oasia when I was a little girl. Always, I have earned my bread by dancing—ever since my first master was slain in a street brawl and I was turned loose to earn my keep."

Red Lori held her palm out to Kothar. The barbarian took two small gold bars from his belt purse, dropped them into her hand.

"Will these buy your freedom and pay your debts?"

Cybala nodded, eyes wide. "That will be more than enough. One such bar will do it."

"Then keep the other, Cybala. Flarion, go with her in case of trouble." Red Lori turned to the Cumberian. "She will please him whom I shall summon up."

"You intend to sacrifice her?" Kothar asked, dismayed.

As if she had not heard him, the witch-woman murmured, "She is a pretty little thing, still young and probably—innocent. Yes, yes, he will like her."

"You can't do it," Kothar rasped, hitting the table.

"Then let us say, we bring her along for young Flarion." Her red lips quirked to a smile in her lovely face as she studied the grim face of the barbarian. "You are a thief, Kothar, a man who has raped his share of women and slain, more than his share of men. Why then, this sudden delicacy?"

He shook his blond head. "I don't hold with human sacrifice."

"Then we'll buy a lamb when the time comes."

He glowered at her, feeling a stab of the old distrust moving in his veins. He had let himself be distracted by her lovely face and ripely curved body. He should have realized that Red Lori was still a witch-woman, a sorceress, no matter how sweetly she acted toward him. Come to think of it, how had she come to be within that tomb, alive and well, as if—waiting for him?

"A demon laid a curse on me," she reminded him, patting his hand with hers when he questioned her. "I told you so before, and now I see you didn't believe me." The fingers tightened, claw-like. "Our sea captain comes, barbarian!"

A brawny man with a scar down his right cheek, his black hair close-cropped about a bullet skull, came swaggering across the floor, striped jersey tight, on a massive chest, his ragged leather sea-breeks tucked into high boots. Around his middle he wore a brass-studded belt from which hung a long dagger and a cutlass. He paused at sight of Red Lori and her beckoning hand, then nodded and moved toward her on catlike feet. He lifted off the mist-wet cloak he wore, dropped it as he crowded his bulk in beside the Cumberian.

"I got your message, I'm Grovdon Dokk of the ship Wave-skimmer The cost will be ten gold pieces"

"Abrupt, and to the point," smiled Lori. "It's a bargain."

"It's robbery," growled Kothar.

The captain looked at him, eyebrows-arched. "Is it yourself or the lady who's hiring me?"

"Pay him, Kothar," smiled the woman.

The barbarian growled under his breath but he did what the witch-woman ordered. "I still say it's robbery, man. Ten gold pieces could buy me such a scow as you probably command. Do you know the seas hereabouts?"

"Better than I know my face," Grovdon Dokk nodded, clinking the golden pieces between his hands and smiling at them. "And I'll have you know I run a tight ship, with accommodations for four guests."

38

"Diving gear?" asked Red Lori.

"And men to dive, if you need them, at no extra cost. I'm a fair man, you'll see. When do we sail?"

"We'll come aboard about midnight." The captain knuckled his brow to the witch-woman and stood up. "I'll go along then, to make things ready. If you could tell me where it is we sail, I could plot a course."

"I'll tell you when we're under way." Kothar watched the sea captain move off with his rolling gait. He growled, "You're cursed mysterious. Why must we keep it such a secret? Is the treasure greater than that of Kandakore?"

"Infinitely greater, barbarian, as you'll learn when you see it." Her smile dimpled her cheeks as her green eyes glowed. "Perhaps it is the greatest treasure in the world."

Flarion was moving toward them, drawing the belly-dancer in his wake with a hand on her wrist. He carried a leather bag, thrown over a shoulder, that bulged with the things Cybala had so hastily thrust into it, which was all she owned in the world. He pushed her onto the bench beside Red Lori just as the serving maid came up with their tankards and a goblet of red Thosian wine.

With them she brought a wooden platter of steaming meat, with wedges of bread and cheese placed around them. Kothar pushed a gold coin at her as he reached for the food.

Cybala whispered, "What am I to do?"

"Amuse Flarion," snapped the redhead.

The girl glanced sideways at the youth, eyebrows arching. Her shoulder lifted and she sniffed, dismissing him. Flarion flushed and stared down at his food.

When the clepsydra showed the hour to be close to midnight, Lori pushed an empty platter away and reached behind her for her heavy woolen paenula. "It is time to go, to board the ship."

Kothar tossed his fur cloak about his massive shoulders, moving ahead of the others so that his giant frame could clear passageway for them between the diners and the revelers. Here and there a hand reached out protestingly when the patrons of the tavern recognized Cybala in a traveling cloak with her dusky face half hidden in its hood.

39

But Kothar was there to push away a hand, and Flarion was close beside the belly-dancer to discourage an overly resentful man with a fist in the ribs or an easily drawn dagger. Cybala walked with heavy steps, half dreading that which she went toward so easily. This going was not of her own will but by force of the green eyes that had looked deep inside her and caught hold of her soul. Only Red Lori went with an easy stride. This was her doing, this night and its events, and those which would follow. Only on her lips was there a smile, and only her feet trod lightly, with satisfaction in the way of their going.

The mists had come in off the Outer Sea, the cobbles and the marble paving slabs were wet with water. The two moons of Yarth were hidden behind dark clouds. The slap of a rising tide against the pilings and the bulkheads echoed the faint pad-pad of their boots as they hastened through the gray fog and the dampness, which the sea wind made swirl about their persons.

Red Lori reached out, caught Kothar by his sword-belt. "Not so fast, Cumberian. We others have not your long legs. It would be easy to get lost in such a fog."

Kothar slowed his pace, letting his thoughts run faster than his feet. He knew the witch-woman was moving on a course that might not be pleasing to him. Yet she had promised to rid him of that curse of Afgorkon by which he could own no treasure but his sword Frostfire. He was a little tired of an empty belly for days on end, when his belt-purse was as flat as his middle. He would relish golden coins clinking in that almoner, and the prospects of hot meals and cold ale every night.

And so he plodded onward through the grayish mists, deeply sunk in reverie, headed nothing but his own troubled spirit, until—

"Haiii!!"

Two men up ahead in the mists, one leaping at another, with the gleam of bared steel in a hand. The second man, tall and lean, shrank back, crying out in dismay.

"Die, damned sorcerer! Into the depths of Eldrak's seven hells with you!"

To see was to act with the barbarian. He lunged forward, glad of this bit of action with which to dispel his gloom. His hand darted out, closed fingers on the wrist of the hard that held the dagger. His muscles bunched, swung the man sideways off his feet and into a building wall.

A face contorted by rage and fear stared at him in horror as the man sought to free his wrist. Haggard eyes half sunken in a skull-like face peered up at the towering barbarian. A thin mouth writhed blasphemies.

"Let me go, fool! I but rid the world of a thing better dead—a misshapen excrudescence of utter evil! Let be, I say!"

"What is it?" gasped Red Lori.

Cybala shrank backward, found an arm about her lissome waist. Her eyes turned sideways, studied the profile of the youthful warrior beside her. His sword was in his hand, there was a faint smile on his lips. Cybala was breathing harshly, leaning her weight deeper into his embracing arm.

He glanced at her; their stares locked. The dagger fell clattering to the cobbles of the narrow alleyway. With a hoarse cry of fear, the man who had held that dagger turned and ran off into the fog. They heard his footsteps pounding, then fading before the surging rush of the surf not far away. The wind moaned as it swept around the corners of these buildings.

The tall, lean man in the black mantle still leaned against the damp bricks of the house wall, breathing harshly. The barbarian bent, picked up the fallen dagger.

"Why did you let him go, Northlander? He was death—that one! Saw you not his face, his eyes?"

Kothar scowled. "Now why should he have tried to kill you? What wrong have you done him?"

"No wrong, not I. For I am Antor Nemillus, mage and necromancer to Midor, King of Sybaros!" He came away from the wall, drawing himself to his full height, his flashing eyes stabbing the mists toward Red Lori and Cybala, and drifting over Flarion for an instant.

His thin lips quirked into a smile as he swung back to the Cumberian. "I owe you a great debt, barbarian. Name your price for your service, and be not humble in your demands—or I'll take it as an insult. The life of Antor Nemillus is worth a kingdom to that man who saves it."

Kothar shrugged, then became aware that a hand tugged at his cloak. He turned, saw Lori oddly shy, almost cowering back into the warmth afforded by the bodies of Cybala and Flarion.

"Safe conduct, Kothar—safe passage for us anywhere in Sybaros and its adjacent waters," she whispered.

Antor Nemillus heard her words and laughed harshly. "Are these my rescuers? More cut-purses with their doxies? Ah, but—no matter. Even a thief can earn a reward for a great service. Here...."

A hand fumbled in a belt pouch, brought out a copper disc inlaid with enamels of varying colors. "My sigil, known the length and breadth of Sybaros, on land and on the sea. It will save you even from—the king's guardsmen. But use it wisely or—it may bring your doom."

The lean man folded the fur mantle about his narrow shoulders and went striding off into the fog. A few moments the barbarian watched him, then those rolling mists hid him from sight. He glanced down at the copper piece he held, studied the intertwined enamels on its surfaces that so much resembled a serpent folded back upon itself.

"The amulet of dread Omorphon," breathed the woman.

"Oh? And will this see us safe against soldiers and lesser wizards?"

"It will. Give it here."

The Cumberian slid the disc into his purse and grinned. "Nay, now. Let me keep it, my red beauty. I'd feel safer with its weight on my person."

She laughed up at him, caught his hand and squeezed it. "Trusting Kothar! Always you see specters where there are none. But come, it moves toward midnight."

They went swiftly through the mists, light reading, and with their cloaks flapping about them as the wind blew more strongly at the pier where Wave-skimmer was docked. A sailor in a striped jersey and ragged culottes was waiting for them beside a crude plank. He steadied the plank as Red Lori and Cybala ran across. When Flarion and Kothar were on deck, he moved across the plank himself, and lifting it, secured it to two pins inset into the fore-rail.

"I'll show you to your cabins," he muttered.

Wave-skimmer as a brigantine. The two masts towered high over their heads as they made their way aft behind the sailor, the sea wind rustling between the yards and snapping the shrouds in their chocks. The salt smell of the sea was everywhere. The ship appeared to sway slightly underfoot as the waves heaved and swelled beneath the keel.

"A rough night," whispered Cybala. The seaman heard her, laughed. "We're still tied to the dock, mistress. Wait until we get out beyond the reefs. There'll be rough water there or I miss my guess."

Cybala moaned, and Flarion took advantage of her momentary weakness to slip an arm about her middle. His own belly was none too steady, he was a landsman, not a deck-swabber. He followed where the others led, enjoying this movement of intimacy with the black-haired dancing girl, the touch of her middle, the awareness of swaying hips that brushed his own her sweet scent and the soft breathing that seemed like music to his ears.

A white door opened, revealing a small cabin lit with a single candle. "Your room, master," he said to Kothar and nodded also at the woman. "With bunks for you and your lady."

Red Lori swept into the chamber, letting her cloak slip onto a table. She took the lone candle in a pale hand, touched its flame to other wicks set here and there. The light flooded the compartment, showed it neat and trim, with two bunks set into opposite walls and a table between, riveted to the wooden bulkhead.

She turned, ripely curved in the leather jerkin and short skirt, and gestured at the sailor before he could close the door. "I'll want to see your captain, Grovdon Dokk. I must tell him how, to set his course."

The barbarian followed her out into the companionway, up a flight of wooden steps and into a cabin set under the quarterdeck. Oil lamps burned brightly as Grovdon Dokk wrote with a scratchy quill pen in his open log.

He glanced up frowning as they entered, but nodded when Red Lori made their mission known. Stepping to a table fitted with boxed compartments, he selected, a scroll and bore it to a table, unrolling it, spreading it out.

"Where away, lady?" A red fingernail scratched the parchment. "Set your course here, captain." His surprised look made her smile. "Yes, it is empty sea. But it is there I would go and—cast anchor."

Grovdon Dokk rubbed his stubbled jaw reflectively. "You pay the fee, I'll not quarrel with you. But it seems senseless lady. To travel to the islands now, or even south into Ispahan, would make more sense."

"To you, perhaps. Not to me. It is there I would go, and where you shall take me." The fingernail tapped the chart imperiously, and Grovdon Dokk shrugged.

Kothar waited until they were in their cabin before he muttered, "I'm of a mind with the captain on this, red one. What do you expect to find on the open sea?"

"Not on, dunderhead. Under!"

His face brightened. "Ah! Sunken treasure. Of course. A ship, eh? A galleass that went down beam-end first in a storm? A treasure ship of King Midor, that was making its way homeward from the spice islands?"

Her laughter rang out as her fingers went to the lacings of her placket. In a moment they were undone, and he caught the sheen of candlelight on creamy skin as the blouse slipped from a rounded shoulder. She preened a little before him, proud of her beauty, her desirability as a woman.

"None of those, Kothar," she said softly. "What we seek has not been seen by men for many thousands of years."

He sat up straighter on the bench where he was easing off his war-boots. "No ship? What, then?"

"The lost city of Hatharon, Kothar. Aye, that city where Afgorkon was born, where he made his spells, where he enchanted the world about him. The greatest magician of them all. Even today, fifty thousand years after Afgorkon lived, his fellow mages revere his name."

She was lifting her short skirt, stepping out of petticoats, thrusting down the velvet placket with the loose lacings. Her body was firmly ripe, so lovely as to make the barbarian feel the tide of his manhood sweep through his veins. Long red hair hung to her hips, her skin was pale satin and gently rounded here and there.

"Girl, I don't understand you," he rasped.

She turned her face, staring at him inquiringly. "You should hate me, by all rights. Since, we met in Commoral in your magic tower,

I've turned your wickedness away from those you'd injure. It was my fault you were hung in a silver cage, and later. I put you into that tomb with dead Kalikalides.

"And—yours isn't a forgiving nature."

Her laughter rang out. "You are mine, barbarian. I've told you that-even while imprisoned in that silver cage. You'll recall how you saw my face in the bottoms of your tankards and peeping out from your campfires? How I talked to you even then?"

"Aye, you said I was yours to do with as you would."

"And you still are." She took the sting from her words by stepping closer, bending to catch his cheeks between her soft palms and setting her red mouth to his. "I think you have always belonged to me, Kothar—even while you were fighting me in my tower, battling the demons and goblins with which I sought to kill you."

"You fire the blood in a man," he rumbled.

Her nimble fingers eased the lacing of his mail shirt, held it so he could slip out of it. She aided him to remove the leather hacqueton he wore beneath the mail, and playfully tweaked the blond hairs on his deep chest. She was like a dutiful wife, he thought, tenderly loving and heedful of his every wish.

He could not still the uneasiness inside him, however, even though he feasted his eyes on her nakedness and his lips tingled to her kiss. This was not like Red Lori; it was as if—she played a part. He would almost rather see the anger-flames in her bold green eyes and hear her soft voice grow shrill with curses on his head. Yet a part of him relished this attention she gave him, even as his body hungered to draw her down between the sheets on one of the bunk-beds

Then he was naked as she and she was clasping his hand, drawing him toward the bunk, bending to blow out the candles one by one until only the moonlight came into the cabin to silver their bodies. Kothar caught her to him, held her close as his mouth feasted on her lips.

They toppled sideways onto the covers.

Some time during the night the barbarian woke to find the ship creaking, dipping to the swells of the Outer Sea as its great sails filled with the blowing winds. The rocking was pleasant to him, snug in this

45

bunk with Red Lori within the crook of an arm. He grinned and drew her even closer. Let the gale moan and the ship lift and fall to the surge of the sea waves, he was content.

Morning was a golden radiance in the cabin as the barbarian threw back the covers and leaped to the middle of the room. Behind him Red Lori squirmed and muttered protestingly as she sought the fallen blankets and drew them closer.

Kothar said as he drew on his kilt, "It's long past dawn, girl. Come share a platter of fish with me."

"Go eat, you big ox. I'd rather sleep," she murmured.

He studied her flushed face, the thick red hair spread on the pillows. By Salara of the bare breasts, she was a woman, this one! Her embraces were all any man might want, her kisses things of fire. Never yet had the barbarian sought to ally himself overlong to any one woman. Those he had known in his wanderings—Miramel and that tavern girl in Murrd, Mellicent, and Laella, who was a dancing girl out of Oasia, and Queen Candara of Kor, and the brunette woman, Philisia, who had been a king's mistress in Urgal—had been but passing fancies, linked with the dust of the lands of their birth, so far as he was concerned.

But with Red Lori, it was different.

He shook his head against what he considered a streak of softness in himself. A sell-sword and wanderer had no time to spare for such sentimental things as love and marriage, nor a family, either. He was a mercenary, with his steel blade he earned his livelihood.

And with the curse of Afgorkon forbidding wealth to him, what sort of woman would even consider him for a husband? Nah, nah. A woman might take him for a lover, but nothing more.

In this frame of mind he went up deck-side, to pause and study the gray sea heaving on all sides. The ship rode easily, its prow cleaving the frothing waves, the white sails bellied outward with the wind. To his surprise he saw Flarion leaning against the starboard rail, staring dead abeam.

He put his hand to the youth's shoulder. "Come join me in a platter of fish, comrade."

"I have no appetite."

"The ship rides smoothly enough."

"It isn't the ship."

"Ah, then it must be the belly-dancer. She wasn't kind to you last night. Did she consign you to your own bunk? And stay in hers until morning?"

"Something like that, yes."

"It's just as well," the barbarian growled. Flarion swung around. "Now what, makes you say that?"

Kothar shook his head. He could scarcely tell the youth that Red Lori had marked the girl for sacrifice to one of her demon-gods. Better to let him suffer now, for a little while, then later when her death would put Cybala forever beyond his reach. He himself did not intend to let the red witch carry out that plan, but he knew her well enough to realize that if her mind were set on Cybala's death, then Cybala would die. He moved off down the deck, his nose telling him where the galley was, the smell of cooking fish stew and broiling fish steak making his mouth water. The oceans teemed with succulent game fish, ripe for eating over hot coals or an oil flame, and few ships that plied the Outer Sea carried more than salt pork and flour and condiments in its food bins. The sea was all around them, and any sailor could dangle a line with a baited hook.

He found half a dozen men at the galley benches, and selected a wooden mug, filled it with the stew, caught up half a loaf of bread and perched his big bulk before a wooden table. He ate voraciously, for his great body needed much food to sustain it, and twice more he filled the wooden bowl before he was content.

He went out on deck and stood watching the sea toss and surge beneath the keel. He felt no sickness, he was like iron in his middle. After a time, Red Lori came to join him, wrapped in her woolen cloak.

The wind blew her red hair free, so that it tickled his face when he bent to hear her words that the same wind threatened to bear away with.

"I say that once there was a continent below our keel, Kothar. Or part of a continent. This sea here covers what was once part of Sybaros and Tharia, a massive plateau that stretched outward for many miles. At its tip, jutting into the ocean, was the port city of Hatharon."

47

"Where Afgorkon was born."

"And where he practiced his wizardries. In what remains of his ancient lodging, in that tower where he kept his chests and scrolls, I hope to find his famous coffer of magic formulas and special incantations."

"And once you've done that?" She looked up at him, laughing. "Then I can free you from his curse, barbarian. And—do what I must do."

"What goal have you set yourself, Lori the Red?"

"To save the magicians of Yarth! Or haven't you heard that someone is slaying them all, very coldly, very systematically? Aye, last night in Zoane, when you rescued Antor Nemillus, was an instance of the wickedness now flourishing in the land."

Kothar scowled. "Why seek you Afgorkon's belongings?"

"He was a wizard. He must help his kind. I would summon him, Kothar, speak with him. If anyone knows how to stop this slayer of sorcerers—he will!"

The barbarian remembered the lich in the hidden tomb within the forests of Commoral, who had given him the sword Frostfire. An unease sat in his middle as he let his memory run on that rotted thing that had been a living man five hundred centuries ago.

"He will not like it," he muttered. "But he will come. Oh, yes. He shall come to my call."

"Only at a price!"

"The girl, Cybala. She will appease him."

"Flarion won't like it," he rumbled. "The boy's half in love with her. He moons over her constantly."

Her green eyes flared. "You think he'd—kill me—to save her?"

The massive shoulders lifted and fell. "You do what you think is right, to save the lives of your fellow sorcerers and wizards. Perhaps Flarion may do what he thinks is right, too."

She bit her lip, frowning thoughtfully. The ship Wave-skimmer ploughed on through the salt waters of the Outer Sea, sails fat with wind, yards and masts straining to those gusts that hurled its prow through the heaving waves. These same salt winds stirred the long blond hair that hung below the barbarian's shoulder, which he tied behind him during battle, and made him draw his thick cloak tighter to his shoulders. He rode the heaving deck on solidly planted war-boots, a scowl on his face.

There were human undercurrents all about him that he did not like. He did not trust Red Lori, for all that he was half in love with her. There was an attitude the witch-woman seemed to have—of waiting, sniffing at the air, like a wolf on the hunt—that made him itch between his shoulder blades. And Florian, half mad himself with love for the belly-dancer, with hate in his eyes when he thought of Red Lori. Ah, and Cybala? He could not read the dancing girl. What emotion gripped her as she lay in her cabin bunk at night?

"We near our goal, Kothar. Look there!"

"A slim forefinger pointed at the waves. Kothar repressed a cry of surprise. These waters were blue, clear as the crystal-ware of Zoardar. And not so far down in those limpid depths-surely those were gardens, he was seeing? He leaned his weight upon the rail, peering downward.

"Aye, barbarian. The pleasure gardens of Afgorkon—or so the legends say Built upon the side of an ancient mountain that did not sink as completely as did all the rest of this land. Here are his artifacts, his impedimenta, the equipment which enabled him to become the most famous wizard of all."

His eyes saw marble statues, rows of dead trees, petrified now, with sea coral and swaying anemones where flowing hibiscus. and lovely roshamores were wont to grow upon a time. He made out something that had been a labyrinth of tall hedges, a stone walkway wending in and out of these once-lovely places, part of a colonnaded temple, shattered and long in ruins.

"It is not so deep here," the witch-woman murmured at his side. "A good diver can fetch to that place and back and bring me what it is I want. Grovdon Dokk. To me!"

And when the captain was at her side, knuckling his brow, "Anchor here! Then send to me your divers," she ordered.

She paced up and down until two dark Tharians, lean men with their nakedness hidden in breech-clouts and belts that held long knives, stood before her. They had deep chests, powerful muscles. Men such as these earned their living off the coral banks beyond the Tharian sea-strand, diving for sponges and occasionally a wreck or two submerged among the bottom stones.

"I seek a chest of many colors," Red Lori murmured, "a coffer in which—hermetically sealed—are certain parchments I would have for my own. It has runes worked onto its top, in bright enamels and rustless metals. You shall know it by its brilliance. It shall draw you as might a lantern lighted below the waves. Fail me not, and two gold bars each shall be your prize."

The Tharians grinned and went to the opening in the railing where a plank was affixed so they could dive deep. Kothar watched them, his eyes moving from them to the waters that appeared oddly cloudy, murky, where the anchor had been dropped. This cloudiness extended outward, hiding the gardens, the statuary and even the columns of the temple to some forgotten god.

The men dove.

Down they went, until they disappeared in that cloudy stirring of the sea bottom, which swallowed them up as if they had never existed. Red Lori went striding up and down the deck, hammering a fist into her palm in her excitement, but the barbarian never moved, never took his eyes from that strange murkiness that seemed so—menacing.

The water-clock dripped away the minutes. Overhead, the sun moved across the sky. It hid behind a cloud and a chill darkness came upon the ship-deck. Kothar stirred. Was the wind moaning? Rising in its intensity? He shivered and looked at Red Lori, bent above the railing, staring into those deeps with worried eyes.

The captain padded across the deck, his face echoing the anxiety in the witch-woman. "They have not come back, mistress. They are good men, strong divers. They have fought undersea things before. I do not like this."

"They have been gone too long," she nodded.

"Shall we up anchor and sail away?"

"No!" The word came out of her in an explosion of breath. Kothar stared hard at Red Lori, seeing tears trickling down her smooth cheeks. There was fright in the green eyes that turned to him, and a desperate appeal for help.

"Kothar! Everything depends on my getting that coffer. Everything!

Including your hope to be free of Afgorkon's curse!"

The big barbarian shook himself. All along, he had known he would be called upon to go down into those eerie deeps, as if a corner of his mind had told him so. He and Frostfire, daring the wrath of Afgorkon: This was what it meant when the chips were on the counting table.

He dropped his cloak, worked loose the leather bindings of his mail shirt. Lori came close, red-nailed fingers striving to loosen clasps. Those fingers trembled and shook so that he was forced to push her hands aside, chuckling.

"Those waters will be cold. Have hot rum waiting for me, well buttered," he grinned, kicking free of his war-boots.

Then he drew Frostfire from its scabbard and vaulted over the rail. He went into the cloudy water, his great chest filled with precious air. The sword dragged him downward until his open eyes caught a blurry glimpse of a ruined marble statue and part of a wall and a stone archway, still standing. Then his bare feet touched bottom.

He must look for brightness, Red Lori had said. The coffer that contained the parchments glowed, she claimed—or so the tale had it. But there was no brilliance here, no hint of any light but that which seeped from the surface. Yet he moved forward, under the arch, eyes darting here and there.

Once, out of the very corner of an eye, he caught a flash of light, but it was blotted out. Yet he swung that way, swam forward toward the tumbled stone blocks of what had been a wall, blue and dim in this sea-bottom world.

And then—

A thing of blackness, ebon and threatening, rose up from those walls, a great jet outline—something bulbous, without shape, unknown and mysterious—and a length of something equally black tugged at his ankle. He fought against it, he lifted Frostfire—slashed.

Frostfire bounced on that rubbery blackness. Another tentacle and another came to wrap around his arms, his torso. Strong were those ebon things twisting about him, like constrictor snakes out of the Oasian jungles. He fought them with his own titanic thews, his muscles bulging, rolling and heaving, trying to slash with his sword-edge, seeking to thrust its sharp point into that rubbery black hide.

51

Kraken1 The vast beast of the sea deeps that dwelt in sea caverns and the long-forgotten ruins that dot the floor of the Outer Sea. A creature large enough to attack a ship, a being of a hundred thick tentacles each able to shatter the mast of a large ship.

He hung helpless in those things as they drew him between a stone archway, past two tumbled statues, toward a black hole in the side of a crumbled stone wall. There was a light ahead of him by which he could see the titanic bulk of the sea beast.

Its maw gaped wide to swallow him.

Chapter Five

Two big eyes stared unwinkingly at him as the ivory beak of the octopus opened wide. Its squat, vast bulk rested against a stone structure that had been an altar, long, long ago. And on the altar was the coffer. Even with his lungs about to burst from lack of air, with his head reeling, Kothar knew the intertwined enamels, the reddish glow of that rust-less metal.

The tentacles brought him upward toward that open maw.

Kothar struggled; he freed an arm, twisted Frostfire, stabbed. The point did no more than prick one of the bulging eyeballs, but the pain must have been sharp, because the tentacles flailed him sideways, away from the terrible beak.

The Cumberian felt stone at his back, crunching into it. He did not see what it was. Some statue or other, he guessed. His right arm went high, holding Frostfire.

Through the water, he heard the faint clang of steel on stone. Instantly, his arm felt the shock of that blow, a quivering began in his fingers that went into his wrist and forearm, then upwards to his shoulder. From his shoulder, that queer tingling ran throughout his body.

And—his flesh began to glow!

Blue he was, all radiant blue—and that body brightness added to the strange light of the enameled coffer. A strength such as he had never known came into his flesh. He writhed in the grip of the tentacles, and strangely felt no more the need for air.

He brought Frostfire down in a sweeping arc.

Against the bulbous head of the great Kraken he drove his steel. The edge went into that blubbery substance, slashing deep. Deep! An inky fluid ran out of the cut. Blood? Purple because of his bluely glowing body and the red blood of the Kraken? Kothar did not know, he wrenched his sword free.

He struck again, again!

Far into that mass he lunged his glowing steel. Whatever had happened—thanks to Dwalka! For now he could fight, he could slay. His barbarian muscles rolled as he struck and cut with the edge of Frostfire until at last its point reached deep inside the Kraken's brain.

The tentacles about him loosed to thrash about, striking the stone walls of what had been Afgorkon's necromantic chamber, long centuries ago. The octopus rose upward, seeking to flee this chamber that was its death room. It reached the archway, quivered, fell atop the lintel stone.

"By Dwalka's war hammer!" thought the Cumberian, sagging against the stone altar. "It was a near thing, that."

His eyes touched the altar, the coffer. From that great strongbox his stare went to the statue behind the altar. It was crudely fashioned, of whitish-blue stone and carven to resemble a man. Perhaps five feet in height, it was little more than a thick stone column with arms and legs cut into its roundness, and a head which was a stone ball set atop the indentations that represented shoulders. It had been that eidolon against which his sword had clanged, filling his body with its eerie power.

The head was faceless. Yet there was a brooding power in the thing, a sense of stone inhabited by something—a god? a demon? a nameless power?—that made the barbarian tense.

This thing had helped him, he told himself. It could not be evil. Yet his barbarian senses shivered as if to the touch of staring eyes. Something, someone, was in that stone and—staring at him.

The water around him was very cold, his blue coloring was fading. He reached for the coffer, gripping it by one of the metal rings set into each end. Coffer in hand, he kicked upward.

He had to swim hard, for the coffer was heavy, and his sword was not so light. He might have made it to the surface quite easily with either the strongbox or the sword, but not with both. Yet enough of that alien strength was in him so that he popped upward into sunlight.

Red Lori leaned across the rail, fifty yards away. At her cry, the longboat was lowered and sailors began to row toward him.

Their hands lifted the coffer onto a thwart. Kothar gripped the moldboard, let himself be towed through the waves toward the ship. The witch-woman herself came to the rail where the plank was fastened, reached down and caught his hand. Flarion was there also, fingers grasping.

He stood on the deck, dripping water. Red Lori handed him a tankard with steaming rum, heavily buttered. He drank deep, draining the mug.

"I almost never came back," he growled as Flarion placed his cloak about his dripping shoulders. "If it hadn't been for a statue down there, an eidolon without a face—"

"Oh!" gasped Red Lori, clutching his arm. "Was it the gift of Belthamquar, the father of all demons? Legend says Afgorkon and Belthamquar were partners in wizardry, fifty thousand years ago. That the demon—father made a faceless idol out of stone, giving it to Afgorkon so that the spirit of the great mage could inhabit it and peer between worlds. . . ."

"I know nothing of that. But when Frostfire hit it as I lifted it for a stroke—I was fighting a great Kraken, it must have been the thing that killed the divers—my body turned blue."

Red Lori made a sign in the air, crying out. "I am a strong man, but never have I been that strong! I glowed like an oil lamp, and my sword did the same. Now I could cut into the Kraken, and I went at it until I slew it."

"It is the eidolon of the demon-father. I know it! You must fetch again, Cumberian. Bring it up to the deck."

"Not I. I've had my fill of watery deeps."

"Please, Kothar! I beg you!" Her green eyes ate at his stare. They seemed to swell, to grow larger and larger. They swallowed him up until he stood in a green haze, helpless and without a will of his own. Strangely, his flesh was no longer cold but warm as if the desert sun baked him.

He nodded, unable to prevent his saying, "I shall go for the statue."

"Now, Kothar! Now!" He turned, without Frostfire and still in that strange-daze, to the rail. His cloak fell from him as he stood on the moldboard and leaped. Once again the waters swallowed him up.

Behind him, Lori made a gesture at two of the sailors. "Throw over a rope so he may make a loop from it. Quickly, quickly!"

Kothar sank swiftly, like a stone. He came down past the limp body of the dead Kraken where it sprawled across the lintel stone, and his bare feet touched the tiles of the dead wizard's chamber. The statue, was where he had left it, brooding across the altar as it had for the past fifty, thousand years. He walked toward it, lifting his hands to clasp its sides.

It weighed heavily, so that he was forced to mount to the altar to lift it even an inch, "I can never rise to the surface with this," he thought. "I'm on a fool's errand."

Then he saw the rope dropping toward him and took it. Making a loop he a fixed it to the statue. He tightened the coil about the eidolon, jerked twice on the rope.

He rose upward, the statue following more slowly.

When he came to the deck, he found half the crew engaged in tugging at the free end of the rope, Kothar grinned, showing his strong white teeth.

"Fifteen men to raise that thing," he said to Red Lori, "and you'd have had me do it by myself. Give me more of the buttered rum."

Cybala went to fetch the tankard with the steaming liquid. The barbarian drank slowly, eyeing the witch-woman. She seemed changed, prouder and more arrogant; her chin was high, her green eyes blazed triumphantly. He felt vaguely disturbed and uneasy.

Then the eidolon was bumping the hull and she ran to direct its lifting, her own hands reaching out to clutch it, keeping it from hitting the ship. Her wise eyes scanned its bluish-white stone when it was placed upright on the deck, her fingertips quivering as they almost caressed it.

"Take it to my cabin," she ordered.

It took ten men with a leather sling to move the statue, to bump it down the companionway and into the cabin Red Lori shared with Kothar. The sailors set up the statue between two bulkhead supports, where a hanging lamp creaked on its chains.

Red Lori sat before the eidolon, chin on fist, studying it. At her feet was the enameled coffer. The barbarian was in a far corner of the cabin, slipping back into his clothes.

"I didn't think it existed," she sighed at last. He came to stand beside her chair, buckling on his sword-belt. "And what are you going to do with it, once you're done with your mooning?"

"It can make me the most powerful woman on all Yarth, barbarian. This eidolon can look across the gulfs of time and space, search out secrets for me that are lost to our mightiest wizards. For the eyes of this thing, and its face, are in the spaces between worlds, in demon lands and magical countries. It can see things no man knows, and report them to me."

He glowered down at her red hair. "And what will you do with such secrets? I believed you were done with wizardry."

She turned her lovely face up to him, and she smiled. "What would you have me be, barbarian—a milkmaid on a farm or a shepherdess on a grassy hillside? No, no. Long ago, ever since I was a child, I have been delving into the books of the necromancers, I have cast spells. I almost gained what I wanted from Markoth, but you prevented that, and Queen Elfa hung me in her silver cage."

She shook her head. "My first problem is to ... but never mind that. Go you and eat. Leave me to my dreams."

With a growl, he went to the galley and ate, and there the captain found him. Grovdon Dokk was a worried, anxious man. He held his seaman's cap in his hands as he flung himself onto the bench opposite the barbarian.

"You look like a good man in a fight, Cumberian," he growled.

Kothar grinned at him, hoisting Frostfire between his legs. "I've done my share and more, true. What enemy do you, expect to meet out here? Pirates from the isles?"

"My crew, man. They're talking mutiny."

Kothar paused with the last bit of bread and sausage halfway to his lips. His blond brows rose. "Mutiny? Now, why should your men rebel against you, captain?"

His thumb jerked over his shoulder. "It's your woman in the cabin, barbarian, That coffer she brought abroad, with the faceless statue, is upsetting the crew, that's what."

"I'll go talk to them."

"Best have that long sword of yours handy when you do. The men are afraid, and frightened men don't reckon odds, Can the lady cast spells?"

"She could, but whether she can now, I wouldn't know."

"Too bad. She might have charmed them with a cantraip or two. As it is—"

A sullen roar broke the stillness of the seas. A woman screamed. Kothar vaulted the table and traced for the door, yanking his steel free as he ran. Up the companionway steps and onto the deck he raced, only to slide to a halt.

Red Lori was being held high above the heads of half a dozen brawny seamen, half naked, the clothes torn from her writhing, struggling body.

"Kothar," she screamed. "Aid me!"

He rasped curses as he leaped forward. "Stay back, mate, yelled a scarred forecastle man.

They dropped Red Lori to the deck, and the scarred man fell to a knee, beside her, dagger out, point touching her soft throat. The Cumberian scraped his war-boot soles on the deck-planks as he game to a stop.

He was helpless, he knew that. For himself, he would have dared a dozen daggers, but he could not risk the witch-woman's life. His fingers tightened on Frostfire's shaft so that the skin showed white above the knuckles as he stared hard at the seaman crouched above Red Lori.

"Let her go, man," he cried hoarsely. "There'll be no magic, no wizardry performed on board this ship if you do. You have my word for it."

The other seamen jeered at him, shaking fists and brandishing daggers of their own. Ugliness glared at him out of their eyes and hard faces.

"The Witch dies!"

"We want no part of her spells!"

"We be honest sailors, we don't hold with deviltry."

Red Lori was very still. Only her eyes were moving, turning toward Kothar where he stood in agonized helplessness on the deck. Those eyes pleaded with him, begged him for rescue. He felt them touch him, appeal for his help.

Think, man. There must be away to save her. At another time, he might have turned away from those green eyes that stared at him so fearfully. But that was when Red Lori had hated him. Now—she felt differently toward Kothar the barbarian. She had lain in his arms, very loving, very affectionate. He could not shake the taste of her kisses, the ardor of her body, from his mind.

"Hand over your sword, mate," yelled a sailor.

"Aye, the sword. Toss it here!"

They clamored, their voices hoarse and savage.

Kothar shrugged. "All right, then—take it!"

He drew back his arms to toss it. But instead of the easy throw they expected, his arm flashed downward. And as his moving arm came down he hurled Frostfire straight at the scarred man. Like an arrow it sped through the air.

Kothar followed it, leaping of his feet. The blade went deep into the chest of the kneeling man. At the same instant, the barbarian slammed into three of the seamen, toppling them backwards. As they went over on their backs, Kothar dodged sideways, barreling into the legs of two men who were bending to sink their daggers into his flesh. His big hands reached out, caught at two legs, yanked their owner sideways and into the bodies of two other seamen.

He was on his feet, big hands balled like clubs and striking as hard. Red Lori was up and running, he saw from the corners of his eyes. A dagger slashed his arm, another opened the flesh of his thigh. In another few seconds he would be buried under men and a dozen daggers would be drinking his blood.

Then the captain was beside him, lashing out with a capstan bar, and Flarion stood on the other side of him, blade darting, thrusting.

Three sailors were down, motionless. Two others were reeling back, hands clutched to wounds, blood seeping between their fingers. The rest gathered into a group, snarling, their own daggers bloody. The captain nursed a slashed chest. Flarion moved the fingers of his sword-hand, all blood red from a cut on his forearm.

"Give them amnesty," called Red Lori from the quarterdeck.

"Never," snarled Kothar. "A boat, captain," cried the witch-woman, leaning across the deck rail. "Allow them the longboat and food. They can reach the coast of Tharia in a good two days and nights."

"A boat, a boat," the men shouted.

"And food Biscuits and meat, with cheese!" Grovdon Dokk nodded his head. "Aye, aye. But what of us, lady? Those of us left aboard can't sail this ship!"

"No matter," shouted a big seaman. The men ran across the deck, bare feet slapping wood, and laid hands on the ropes and davits from which hung the single lifeboat of the brigantine. An instant later, with a creak of pulleys and the hum of cording, it was swaying downward toward the water. Kothar stared at the men, tumbling over one another in their eagerness to get down into that boat.

Three of the more longsighted of the crew ran to the galley, carrying back sacks filled with meat and bread, and a few wine-skins. Cook was with them on their last trip, the barbarian noted.

Then oars were being shipped and the longboat was pulling away through the waves, lifting and dropping. A ragged cheer went up from the throats of the men crowded from its prow to the rounded stern. Grovdon Dokk watched them go, and spat to windward.

"Cursed rebels," he snarled and glanced at the dead bodies littering his deck. "I have to give them proper burial," he muttered.

"Flarion and I will help," the barbarian offered.

All that afternoon they sewed canvas sacks to wrap about the bodies of the four dead men. Toward sunset, as the captain read from the Book of the Ten Gods, one by one Kothar and Flarion let the bodies slip into the sea, weighted down by leaden balls. Cybala came to stand in the after deck companionway, wrapped in her paenula, eyes dark and brooding, but Red Lori was nowhere to be seen.

The ship was still anchored above the house and gardens that had been Afgorkon's, long ago. It was motionless here, becalmed, as the moon rose, and flooded the glass-like surface of the waters with its silver radiance.

Grovdon Dokk muttered to the barbarian, "I don't like this stillness, it isn't natural. I begin to wish I'd gone with the others. And how are we to sail Wave-skimmer, two landsmen and myself? Will you tell me that?"

"I can't guess," Kothar muttered. He was tired. It had been a hard day, what with his diving and that fight with the Kraken and bringing up the coffer by himself; and later, quelling the mutiny before Red Lori got herself killed, and then stitching up the death bags. He would sleep well enough tonight, by Dwalka! Yawning, he nodded at the captain.

"I'm going to find my bunk," he said. "I'd advise you to do the same."

"Who can sleep? This is my ship, barbarian. I make my living with it. And she's stuck out here, nine miles from Kantar shoals, with never a bit of breeze to flap her sails. I don't like it. Maybe the men were right, maybe that redhead is a witch with a curse on her head."

"She isn't. Wouldn't she have used a spell to free herself from the sailors, if she were a witch?"

Grovdon Dokk rubbed his stubbled jaw. "May-hap, And may-hap not. I'm an honest man and honest men don't know which way a witch's mind runs."

The Cumberian moved along the deck to the companionway. As he passed their cabin door, he heard Cybala and Flarion, arguing. Like husband and wife, he thought. He felt like yelling to the mercenary to throw the girl on a bed and take her and be done with it. It was probably the only sort of argument she really understood.

His big hand turned the knob of his own cabin door. Red Lori crouched before the eidolon, parchments spread across her knees and tossed helter skelter on the cabin floor. She frowned, staring at the words written on those scrolls, and her lips moved from time to time as she sought to understand their meanings.

"Sleep wouldn't hurt you, either," he growled, getting out of his mail shirt. Seeing she ignored him, he crossed the worn carpeting to peer down over her shoulder.

"You're in my light, Kothar. Go to sleep."

"Can't you read, witch-woman?" he jeered. She looked up at him. "Not this script, not easily. The language in which these parchments are written is fifty thousand years old. There have been some changes since then."

"I thought you sorceresses knew all those ancient languages."

"We know some, yes. These are very old. But I begin to understand them, a little. It is slow going at first. It will go faster, very soon."

61

Kothar stretched, yawning. He kicked off his war-boots, sitting on the edge of his bunk. Red Lori was lost to him for the night, he could see that. She was bent above those scrolls as if they contained the secret of life and death for her.

Maybe they did, for all he knew. He slid into bed in his under breeks and quilted hacqueton and drew the blankets up to his neck.

In moments, he was asleep. He dreamed he stood in a blue mist, shivering with cold. The mist was speaking to him, whispering strange and "troubling words, the meaning of which he should understand and did not. Red Lori was calling out to him, very faintly, or perhaps she spoke those words; he could not tell. He called her name and began walking slowly through the blue mist.

She ran toward him, covered all over with icicles and hoarfrost tinkling to her every stride.

She was weeping bitter tears and as he opened his arms to draw her close, a sharp icicle gouged his flesh.

He woke up.

He was not in the cabin, he was inside a tomb.

The sweat came out, on his sun-browned face. "There was blue light everywhere, demon-light such as had lit the mausoleum of long-dead Kalikalides. Now what made him think of that tomb in far-off Xythoron? As his eyes became more accustomed to the azure radiance, he saw a stone bier and on it a body clad in purple and gold garments. It was the body, of a young—

No, by Dwalka! The body had only the similarity to youth. This was the mage Kalikalides himself, kept eternally young by certain necromantic spells. Its cheeks were flushed, its lips red as if with life. And standing in a corner of this vault—Red Lori!

But wait. If that was Red Lori, who was it who stood naked to one side of his bed, a parchment scroll in a hand, chanting words unheard on Yarth for fifty thousand years? It too, was the witch-woman.

"Gods of Thuum," he breathed. For Red Lori was singing, and the other Red Lori, the one in the dark corner, clad in the blouse and fringed skirt of the Mongrol plains woman, was floating toward her double. Her feet did not touch the ground, it was as if she drifted between worlds. There was a nimbus of light about her and her eyes were wide and staring, yet she came nearer to the redheaded woman with the parchment scroll, nearer, nearer!

The barbarian shivered, aware of some vague voice in his mind bidding him leap to prevent the joining of these two woman-shapes. There was danger here, dread danger, of a kind he did not know, being no sorcerer. Yet he felt it with his animal senses.

"Red Lori," he croaked. "Give over your wizardries!"

She paid him no heed, but went on chanting. Now Kothar could see the outlines of objects inside the cabin, the eidolon close to the bulkhead, the lamp hanging from its chain nearby and under it, bathed in its light, the coffer with the enameled sigils on its top. Aye, and the bunk where the witch-woman was wont to sleep when she was not sharing his own, and the shirt of mail and his war-boots where he had discarded them.

The tomb was here, as well, the bier plain to see, and the body on it. There was a blending of two spaces, the barbarian realized, the tomb and the cabin. He was here on the Outer Sea, yet he was inside the black crypt of the dead magician.

He did not understand how this could be, except by necromancy. His eyes saw the decorations on the mausoleum, his nose smelled the charnel odors of the grave, his ears heard Red Lori singing.

The other witch-woman floated closer, closer. Soon they would join, these women who were but one.

The cold sweat stood out on Kothar's forehead. He reached for Frostfire, but in this double-space his fingers could not grip its shaft. He sat here on the bed, but his sword was forbidden him.

And so he watched.

The Red Lori in the Mongrol garb touched the naked Red Lori. Her hand went into and around that other hand, as her shoulders and hips became one with her simulacrum. Legs and breasts and belly, the two women merged together.

The cabin was warm, suddenly. Gone was the grave chill, the noisome smells, the dampness. A fire glowed in an iron brazier and by its light, and the radiance of the lamp above the coffer, Kothar could see Red Lori clad in the tattered Mongrol garments she had worn when he had sealed her inside the crypt in Xythoron.

She turned and, laughing softly, saw him watching her.

"Aye, Kothar! I am—myself! Free of the mausoleum where you imprisoned me. A live! and—free!"

"You've been free ever since I took you out of Kandakore's tome."

"No, barbarian—no! It was only my image which has traveled with you these past weeks.

My astral self, which I drew from another plane of existence and brought into our own."

He glowered at her. "So that's why you wanted the coffer. It wasn't to free me from any curse of Afgorkon, not at all."

Her white fingers went into her long red hair, lifted it high above her head as she pivoted, dancing a few steps about the cabin. Her laughter rose upward, softly mocking.

"I am myself, I am Red Lori," she sang. "And Kothar is my slave!" She pointed a red-nailed finger at him. "Yes, barbarian. You are mine, you belong to me. We are not finished, you and I. I have a further need for your big muscles and your magic sword."

"You can't command me. I—"

"Ah, but I can. I can, Kothar! Before I could not, my astral image lacked the power-which explains why I was so sweet to you, so loving. I twisted you about my little finger, I gave you kisses and—more than kisses—to make certain that you were no more than a love sick fool!"

He sought to rise from the bed; could not. It was as if invisible chains held him motionless. "You see?" she cried gleefully. "I possess many of my old powers, now. There is no need to wheedle and cajole. No longer!"

She came across the floor on light feet. Her hand slapped his cheek, back and forth. His head rocked to her blows. Between her teeth, she snarled, "I am your mistress You are my slave! My slave, Kothar the mighty! You are less than a lapdog, no stronger than a midge—without me.

"Oh, yes. You shall obey me. Without question, without argument. When I say run, you shall run. If I say kill, you and that sword of yours shall kill in my name. You cannot help yourself."

She stopped hitting him, brought her hand to her mouth and licked its smartings with her tongue, her green eyes impish as they regarded him. She smiled suddenly and held out her stinging palm, reddened from her repeated slappings of his cheeks.

"Kiss it," she ordered. And Kothar touched his lips to her flesh. His soul writhed in his body, but he was helpless against her green eyes and her powers. There was an aura about her, much like that blue nimbus in which his body had been clothed when Frostfire had struck the eidolon in time to save his life beneath the surface of the Outer Sea. He could not resist it, nor her commands.

She ruffled his blond hair, suddenly. "Oh, I'll treat you well, for the most part. A master is good to a valuable slave. You are valuable to me, Kothar. So I shall be good to you."

Red Lori turned away, moving with swaying hips toward the cabin door. She opened the door, walked out. Kothar felt the thralldom fall away from him. With a snarled oath, he bounded , from the bed, snatching up Frostfire. He ran for the doorway and into the narrow passageway. On bare feet he raced up the companionway and out upon the deck. The witch-woman stood with upraised arms, the sea wind toying with her hair. Her eyes were raised to the clouds scudding across the sky, through which the two moons of Yarth peeped, round and silvery like demon eyes. There was a faint radiance about her body, a bluish glow that snapped and crackled to the ears in the stillness of the night.

"Io k'harthal mollonthal! Pthond kathondal pha benth." Her voice rose up in a series of ululating sounds that made the short hairs rise on his neck. There was an eerie quality to her voice. Those sounds seemed made not by human vocal chords but by those of some alien being; they held Kothar paralyzed.

"Great god Poseithon, whose breath comes to our world as wind and gale and storm, heed my prayer! Io k'harthal mollonthal! Send your breath to me, to this corner of Yarth, according to my need. And gently honored be thy name, lord Poseithon!"

There was a distant moan in the night, a faint whisper of sound that stirred the waves in tiny ripples on either side of the brigantine. The barbarian could see Grovdon Dokk crouched on the main deck, staring at the woman encased in the crackling blue glow. The Wave-skimmer had lain becalmed. The surface of the sea around them had been glassy, still as any woods pond. Yet now the ripples grew larger,

larger, and the ship lifted to the waves that formed. It rose gently, fell easily. And the moan grew louder, louder.

A breeze brushed Kothar, stirring his golden hair, ruffling the fur that trimmed his kilt, The wind was warm, heavy with exotic scents from the Southlands, almost musky. Above his head the riggings rattled and the sails shook weakly. The breeze became a wind, filling the sails. Grovdon Dokk cursed faintly, stirred from his position and ran up the after-deck companionway. The helm was swinging idly, turning this way and that as the waves caught it, as the canvas filled and drove the ship forward. His big hands went to the whip-staff, caught and held it. Forward surged the ship on a steady course, its prow cleaving the gathering waves with a faint gurgle of rushing waters.

The blue radiance faded. Red Lori let her arms drop. She stood a moment head-bowed, as if exhausted. Then she lifted a hand, brushed fallen locks of red hair from her eyes. She turned, saw Kothar; stood still, smiling faintly.

"We go to Zoane," she said softly. "On the way, I shall prepare the necessary spells that will animate the eidolon. Come you with me, barbarian."

Her green eyes looked at him as she spoke; they were enormous, staring. He had no will to resist them. He nodded and waited until she crossed the deck-planks to fall into step just behind her.

The cabin was lighted by the single lamp hung on chains from the beamed ceiling. In its golden glow the faceless eidolon stood silent, ominous. The barbarian felt the mute menace of that grim statue, his flesh crawled at the thought of what it represented.

Red Lori crossed the cabin floor, lifted a parchment from the coffer. Unrolling it, she knelt before the eidolon. Softly she began to read from the ancient writings. The room grew cold, there was a smell of the grave and rotting cerements in the air. Kothar growled and put his hand on Frostfire.

To the Cumberian, the statue seemed to writhe in protest, to move its stubby arms and legs. It was a trick of the light, he told himself, for the ship was rising and falling to the surging waves as it cleaved a path toward Zoane.

A whisper in the air touched his ears. "Who calls Afgorkon? Who comes to disturb his sleep after five hundred centuries?”

“I call, great mage, lord of the fifty worlds of Kafarr, worlds of your own creation I seek your help for your brother magicians, victims of assassins in this land of Yarth; which you knew long ago.”

There was a silence. The whisper came again. “I feel pity, for my brothers in magic. Yet Afgorkon has withdrawn himself from those lands which once knew his name."

“His name! This is all I ask, great wizard. Peer into the astral planes surrounding our own. Speak his name only—and leave the rest to me. And to my man-slave, Kothar!”

"Ah, Kothar. Is he with you? Yes, I see him—and his sword Frostfire, which was forged in the primal ooze by certain—devils—of my acquaintance. How like you the sword, barbarian?”

“I like it,” said Kothar. Afgorkon chuckled. "Aye, even though with it, you are pauper! I see it in your eyes. your blade is the only thing in life you love.” There was a little silence, then the mage breathed out words again in that hoarse voice, faint with far distances. "I shall look as you desire, woman who has waked me. Not for you, but for the sake of those who are my kin in warlockry.”

Red Lori still knelt, and now she leaned forward, touching her forehead to the base of the eidolon, crying, "My thanks, great mage!”

The cabin was still. Kothar realized that the face of the eidolon was not here in this world, but in those many-faceted lands that surround Yarth in which the demons dwell, and those of the elder race of gods in which are reflected, like objects in a dark glass, the deeds done in his world. Long the eyes of Afgorkon looked, long was the silence in the cabin.

“I see death,” said the voice of Afgorkon. "Death from the rusted daggers and rotting swords of those who have gone before. Up from their graves they have been summoned by dire spells, to slay such mages as are marked for death by him who would destroy them.”

“His name, great Afgorkon? His name?"

"I know not his name. Nor do I see his face in these other megacosms through which my eyes wander. He had protected himself by mighty enchantments against such knowledge becoming known.”

Red Lori wailed, “Then how may I stop him?”

"Go you to those other warlocks whose lives are threatened. Gather them together, induce them to perform spells: I will aid them—if I can. The assassin has enlisted powerful forces against us. How he protects himself from my eyes, I do not know—but I will attempt to learn."

The voice died out.

Red Lori rose slowly from her knees, and in the lamplight her face seemed haggard, worried, as she turned it toward the barbarian. "I was sure he could tell me, I was so sure of it! Now . . ." Her shoulders rose and fell in resigned despair.

"If this means so much to you, why not follow his advice? Go to the magicians who are threatened, employ their help."

She stared at him coldly. "If Afgorkon cannot help, how can they who are not one-tenth the magician he was—and is—in those fifty cosmic lands of his?"

"What have you to lose? Besides, Afgorkon may help you."

She considered him with her stare, nodding at last and sighing. "It may be, yes. If the mage will tell us where the wizards have hidden themselves, then I may send you to them as my emissary, to cajole them into meeting with us and using our combined wisdoms."

Her palms clapped together as if to show that her mind was made up. She swung to the coffer, sorted through the parchments there. Nodding, she selected one, unrolling it and glancing over it at the barbarian with a faint smile.

"I lack many of the magical impedimenta of my black tower, Kothar. But one of these spells will do nicely, along with that scepter I removed from the tomb of Kandakore. It has certain—ah—properties, this scepter."

She lifted it from where it lay beside the coffer and made cryptic signs in the air with it, saying softly, "I shall call on Afgorkon to help me send you to find one of those wizards who are hiding from the world, terrified of the assassin's dagger."

Red Lori began to chant in that same thick voice which she had used on deck when she had summoned up the father of winds. At the same time she went on moving the scepter in the air.

The room grew cold. The barbarian found himself staring at the shimmering outlines of the cabin that shifted and grew hazy, as if the cabin and the woman were fading to invisibility.

Kothar felt a wrench in all his muscles.

Chapter Six

He stood on a vast plain beneath a red sun, amid a scene of awful desolation. Instinctively he knew this was a dying world, perhaps he had been cast through uncountable millennia to those days before the end of Yarth. There were low rounded hills in the background, eroded by wind, rain, and age. The ground underfoot was almost sand, so fine it was, and only here and there were any living plants.

Yet it was not this wasteland that filled him with awe. Rather, it was the dozen or more glowing signs—suspended in the air, blazing as if with fire, though there were no flames—that made a low, moaning noise as the wind blew through them. There was a feeling of strange energies in the air, magical energies, that made the sweat come out onto his forehead.

The barbarian shook himself. His hand touched Frostfire, wrapped fingers about it. This was where one of the warlocks of Yarth had hidden himself thousands—perhaps even millions—of years in the future. His spells had carried him through space and time, just as Red Lori had. sent him, Kothar, to find this man.

He walked forward below the burning signs. They did not halt him nor even slow him down for their magic was not directed against a living human such as he, but only against the assassins from the grave who served the killer-mage's dread will.

He had not far to go before he saw the seated figure. This man was old, with white hair framing a bald head, his face covered with a long white beard. He looked up as the sand grated under Kothar's war-boots, and his dark eyes were big with terror. His pale, trembling hands came up as if to push the Cumberian away.

"No,"he wheezed. "No, no..."

"I'm no killer," growled Kothar. "I've been sent by Red Lori and Afgorkon to help you."

"Afgorkon?" The bald head went up, the old nostrils flared. "Aye, if any can help, he might."

Kothar spoke of the eidolon and of the enameled coffer that contained the lost arcana of the mage Afgorkon. The old man's excitement grew until he was almost dancing in his eagerness and renewed hope.

"It may be, it could be. It's worth a chance, the risk surely. Ah, to mingle my spells with those of fabled Afgorkon. It would be the supreme triumph of my long life."

He added, "Wait I will take us back to Red Lori with a spell of my own and—"

The air seemed to burn around them. The sigils hanging in the air blazed more brightly, glowing scarlet. And the old man screamed in stark terror.

Kothar swung around. Coming across the plain in great leaps and bounds were three half-rotting corpses. One was so frayed by time and the grave that it seemed little more than a skeleton bound together by brown, withered ligaments. And it carried a rusted battleaxe in a hand.

"The liches that serve the assassin," sobbed old Phordog Fale. "Nothing can stop them. Run now, barbarian-while you can still save your life. They don't want to kill you, unless you make them. They care only about me!"

Kothar rasped, "By Dwalka! Red Lori sent me to fetch you to her— and I mean to do so."

He leaped, his sword-blade sparkling in the red fury of the blazing sigils above his head. They were being consumed too fast, he understood that; in some manner the killer must have found a way to counteract their protective magic by causing them to burn themselves up. He ran to meet the oncoming corpses with a snarl on his lips.

The steel blade swung. A rotted head leaped from its shoulders. Kothar whirled, slashed at a second, driving his steel between bones and putrid flesh. The liches never halted in their running; dead men all, they could not be killed a second time.

The barbarian swore, his flesh creeping. The old man was behind him, patiently waiting for the death he felt he could not avoid.

They were past Kothar now, with eyes only for Phordog Fale. The Cumberian grinned coldly and ran after them. He ran lightly, swiftly, soon overtaking them.

Now he drove Frostfire in a savage arc so that its edge would bite through thighbones and dead flesh. One lich fell to the ground, and then a second. They tried to run on the stumps of what had been legs but made only slow, snail-like progress.

He caught the third corpse as it was swinging its rusted ax high to bring its edge down at the old man. Frostfire sliced through the rotting wooden handle of that ax; the ax-head fell to the ground. The lich whirled, dove for Kothar with its bony hands up to claw.

Kothar cut its arms off. Then he slashed at its legs until it was no more than the torso of a dead man flopping on the ground. He turned to the others that still crawled across the ground. Their arms he hacked off, he cut them into gobbets with his steel.

Panting, he paused to glance at the stunned Phordog Fale. "Old man, chant that spell of yours that will get us out of here before somebody sends more dead men for me to slice apart."

The old man began his incantation. In seconds, they were in the cabin of the Wave-skimmer Red Lori cried out delightedly at sight of the old man. "Phordog Fale! I haven't seen you since I was a little girl at the court of King Zopar, where you were chief magician. Do you remember me?"

The old man smiled as he caught her hands. "Dear Lori with the red hair, I mind you well. Always you were under my elbow, practicing my spells, memorizing the various cantraips. When you were alone you pored over my books on magic, learning them word for word. And now you have saved my life."

"You must help, Phordog Fale. Alone, it is too much of a task for me." She went on to speak of the finding of the coffer and the statue, and of what Afgorkon had told her.

Kothar watched and listened for a few moments, but there was a need in him for clean, fresh sea air. He did not care for the stinks of magic and dead bodies. He went up onto the deck where he stood with the salt wind blowing lazily and the ship swaying and dipping as it ploughed through the waves.

He turned his head, saw Grovdon Dokk like a statue at the whip-staff, cloak flapping in the winds. He wondered at the thoughts of the sea captain, with his great ship running before a wizard wind. It was probably not the first time in his life that he had come in contact with sorcery.

He called up to the man. "How soon to Zoane, captain?"

"A day and this night, barbarian. Tomorrow at sundown we anchor in its harbor." Grovdon Dokk spat into the wind. "I like it not, this traveling by a wind that shows itself only on the ship. Look you at the sea."

Gone were the ripples that had appeared at this first onrush of breeze. Now the sea was calm as if Wave-skimmer lay in the tropic doldrums. Kothar shrugged. After what his eyes had seen, this glimpse of working magic was as nothing. He went down the companionway with a wave of the hand at the bemused sailor.

Red Lori waited in the cabin, where old Phordog Fale rested his aged body on a bunk. The witch-woman snapped at him, "Where were you? I have need for you."

Kothar thought of his advice to Flarion. Perhaps he ought to throw this one down on a bunk too, and take her; it might teach her manners. Perhaps she read his intent in his face, for she lifted her chin like an empress, saying, "You would not dare! I would blast you with a dozen curses, leave you naught but a babbling idiot."

"Is this why you summoned me?"

"I have a task for you. Phordog Fale has told me that Nemidomes of Abathor has also taken refuge against the magicks of the killer-mage. You will go to him, bring him back with you."

"Girl, my belly aches with emptiness. I'll—" She was crying out the words and the wrenching was in his muscles, agonizing. Under his war-boots the cabin floor tilted oddly as she moved the scepter this way and that in the air.

He stood on the cobbled floor of a tunnel. All around him were bluish-purple walls, seemingly carved out of rock and dirt, rounded and abandoned. To his left were clay cylinders tumbled and shattered. Ahead of him he could make out a reddish light, oddly flickering. The barbarian sighed and began his walk. Somewhere up ahead he would discover Nemidomes of Abathor, he was certain.

His war-boots were dusty by the time he came to the end of the long tunnel way, and now he could hear the sound of voices murmuring softly and smell the odors of natron and balsalm. He came to a stop, eyes striving to pierce the purplish gloom of this rock-walled chamber. He knew what it was, a charnel house where the dead of Abathor were stuffed with quick lime and bitumen for the better preservation of their corpses. Of all the lands of Yarth, only Abathor spent so much care and money on the preservation of their dead.

His eyes roamed, seeking the shape of him who might be Nemidomes. Most of the men at whom he stared were scrawny, aged beings whose skin was purple because of the spices and unguents which they handled day after day. Among them would be one whose skin was pink. He began walking forward.

It was one of the corpses that betrayed Nemidomes. For the Cumberian saw a dead woman sit up—she had been stabbed in a quarrel, he gathered, because there was a dagger still sticking between her ribs—and yank out that dagger and hurl herself without a sound toward the back of a plump man with shaggy gray hair.

Kothar cursed and leaped. His arms went around the legs of what had been an attractive woman short hours before, but was now cold, dead flesh. His stomach turned over as he felt that dead flesh against his own. But his hand stabbed out, grasped the lifeless wrist, and hammered it against a cobblestone.

The body writhed and twisted in his arms as it fought him savagely. It did not breathe, being dead, yet it was seemingly alive, making it the more ghastly. Teeth bit into his arm, nails scratched. Kothar grunted, reached up, a hand to tangle fingers in long hair and battered that lifeless skull upon the stones: Again and again he hammered the head to the stone until bone cracked. Still the thing fought on.

He ripped out Frostfire, struggled to free himself, made it to his feet. The sword flashed, and as the steel sheared through the dead flesh and bone, the thing flopped across the cobbles. Nemidomes was panting in terror, watching. The charnel workers were gathered in a circle surrounding the dead thing, crying out in horror. When he was done with Frostfire, the corpse was in many parts, all of them wriggling and twisting. Kothar stared down at what was left of that which had been a woman and wanted to be sick. He fought the sickness, waiting until the necromantic life which had sustained if faded away and nothing remained but truly lifeless flesh.

Then he reached out and caught Nemidomes by a wrist. As the sorcerer shrank from him, the barbarian drew him nearer to his whisper. "I come from Red Lori and from old Phordog Fale! I'm here to save you from the assassins!"

The plump little man was covered with sweat all over his pink face.

He shook in his fear and resisted only slightly when the Cumberian dragged him down one of the tunnel ways.

"I t—thought I was so s—safe," he babbled, running a hand across his face, trotting where the big barbarian led, "hiding in the ch—charnel house. I d—didn't realize whoever is trying to ki—kill us magicians is using the d—dead to do it!"

"Well, he is," rasped Kothar, turning to look down at the little man. "Have you any idea who it is?"

Pale blue eyes stared back at him hopelessly as the plump man shook his head, making his jowls jiggle. "No. I thought you mi—might, since you got here in time to save my life."

"You'd better make a spell to get us out of here." He told the magician where the Wave-skimmer was located.

The smaller man made some passes with his hands, chanted a few words. In a moment the tunnels were gone and the familiar deck of the brigantine was underfoot. The magician sighed and his shoulders sagged.

Then his worry came back and he stared around him with fretful eyes. "We aren't safe even here, you know. The assassin can see us. That's how he knew I was in the charnel house."

And that Phordog Fale was hiding at the end of the world, the barbarian thought to himself. He caught the plump man by an elbow, brought him down the companionway to the cabin where Red Lori and Phordog Fale were waiting.

Red Lori said to Kothar, "Phordog Fale and I have been busy since you left to find Nemidomes. We have spoken to Kazazael of Commoral, to Ulnar Themaquol, to Kylwyrren of Urgal. We have decided to band together, to apply all the magicks each of us knows to throw a barrier around ourselves?"

Kothar shrugged. The green eyes sharpened. "You will bring Flarion and the dancing girl. We leave at dusk. Horses will be ready at the quay, where Grovdon Dokk has gone to arrange these matters."

The barbarian found, Flarion on deck, with Cybala across the ship from him, staring at the waters of Zoane harbor. His thumb jerked back at the quarterdeck cabin.

"They'll need protection," rasped the barbarian, "They're great magicians, all of them, but they're about as helpless as babies when it comes to standing of a dagger or sword attack. This will be our job."

Flarion snarled, "I want no more to do with it. What've we gotten out of this, Kothar? Not so much as a copper soldan! And what've we got to look forward to? Just hard fighting. I say leave the redheaded woman and her wizards to shift for themselves."

"The Cumberian grunted. "You have the girl."

"Pah!" Flarion spat over-side. "That one cold as a northern sea, by Salara! She almost ran a dagger into me when I sought to kiss her last night."

"And what did you do? Take the dirk away from her and beg her pardon? Boy, you're an idiot where a skirt's concerned."

The youth looked uncomfortable. "Just the same . . ."

"We stay. Who knows, maybe you'll make the wench like you yet." He chuckled, eyeing his friend. "You want me to speak to her?"

Flarion looked suspicious. "What are you going to say?"

"I'll send her running into your arms. Just let me handle it my way and don't interfere. Agreed?"

Flarion nodded slowly, and watched the big barbarian cross the deck toward the larboard rail, where Cybala leaned her weight. He saw Kothar catch the hood of her long cloak and pull it back, freeing the glossy black hair of the dancer so that it rippled down her back.

Cybala turned on Kothar like a spitting cat. The Cumberian grinned and grabbed her hair, half lifting her of her feet. The pain was excruciating, and she screamed.

"Save your breath, wench," he growled. "Or I'll bang your head on the railing to teach you manners. I just want a look at you."

He yanked open her cloak, revealing her curving body clad in a short purple tunic that displayed her ripe flesh. She gasped, sought to close the woolen paenula.

"Ease off, girl. Red Lori says Afgorkon will want you as a human sacrifice, I say he won't. I just want to see what he's going to get. After all, he's a patron of mine."

"Afgorkon?" she whispered. "A human sacrifice?"

"The fabled necromancer, yes. He's been dead fifty thousand years, but he still lives. Of course, they'll have to kill you to get you to him—he lives in a world of his own making into which no living person can go. You have to be dead to go there."

The girl went white. Her knees shook so that she had to lean against the railing to stand erect. She whimpered, "You're only jesting. Say you're jesting, Kothar!"

He shook his head. Not I! Nor does Red Lori. Why do you think we brought you along, wench? What need have we of a belly-dancer except as a human sacrifice to Afgorkon?"

"No," she breathed. "No!"

"I say he won't take you, but we'll never know until you're dead. Too bad, I say. Flarion seems to think highly of you. Why, I don't know and can't guess—but he does."

"Flarion," she whispered, turning her head to look across the deck.

"Don't look to him for help," he told her, and left to walk across the deck toward the companionway.

He grinned as he heard the padding of her slippers as she ran across the planks to the starboard rail where the young mercenary leaned. Turning at the companionway, he saw her clinging to his arm, pleading, lovely face upraised.

He was turning away when his eyes caught sight of a bright shaft of sunlight some miles away. Its blinding brilliance hurt the eyes. This was no result of any sun This was sorcery. He watched it squinting for a few seconds, then rounded on a heel and dove down the companionway.

He came into the cabin like a whirlwind. "On deck, the lot of you," he growled, waving an arm, "There's a beam of light coming this way—straight for the ship."

Nemidomes cried out sharply. Red Lori made a little gesture with a hand, pushing past the barbarian who swung to follow her. As she came up onto the deck planks she shaded her eyes with a hand, staring northward.

"Aye, it's wizardry," she nodded. "Do you have a spell to counter it?" Phordog Fale and Nemidomes were on the deck, staring where the witch-woman looked. It was the plump little man who muttered, "A demon light. There are ways to counteract it but without my scrolls and palimpsests, I'm helpless."

"I'm not," snapped Red Lori, and bent to duck past Kothar.

Phordog Fale was twisting his pale hands together, face crumpled by fright. Beside him, the little man was sweating profusely, the fear of something worse than death in his eyes. The Cumberian snarled and moved around them to go to the cabin after the redhead.

She was kneeling before the eidolon, head bent, whispering almost to herself. He stood in there.

". . . destroy us before we . . . your power and strength only can . . . must aid us, Afgorkon. . . the assassin will slice the boat in half, burning us all in flames of demonry . . . save us . . . to save the lives of . . ."

As he watched, Kothar caught his breath. For a moment, the faceless stone appeared to shimmer faintly, and he saw eyes in that stone and a face where a face should be. He shivered. These were not the features of the dead lich that had been the Afgorkon who had given Frostfire to Kothar. This was the face of a youthful sorcerer, proud and hard.

"I see the demon light, it comes out of the seven hells of Eldrak. The sorcery aligned against you and the others is very great, Red Lori. And you are right. That light will burn your ship and everything on it to a cinder!"

Kothar shivered. Red Lori wailed, "Save us!"

"I call upon Belthamquar, father of demons. I summon Eldrak, who has permitted this light to be stolen from his seven hells!"

The voice was strong, like a gale off the northern glaciers. The room was very cold, suddenly. And in that cold, even while he drew his cloak closer about his great shoulders, Kothar thought to see a redly flaming figure standing beside the eidolon. Eldrak of the seven hells? And on the far side of the statue, another demon, Belthamquar!

"Who calls Eldrak?"

"And Belthamquar?"

"I call," came a voice from the eidolon. "I, Afgorkon, friend to you both. Is this the will of Eldrak, of the demon father? Are all the wizards of Yarth to be slain by a common murderer? Even now a demon light swirls down upon the ship."

"I see it," breathed Eldrak excitedly. "It does come from my burning worlds! But—by what right? I gave no permission!"

"Then stop it," snapped Belthamquar.

Eldrak lifted his hands, cried out thickly, half a dozen words that seemed to sear the very air around him. The barbarian heard voices shouting on deck. He could not make them out, but he realized they were cries of relief, of delight. Apparently the demon light was being recalled back into the seven hells out of which it had been summoned.

Cold chills ran down Kothar's back as he stared at these demon lords, these gods of space and time, at their shimmering figures flanking the eidolon and the kneeling, trembling witch-woman. Vaguely he understood that Red Lori had called upon tremendous forces and that she was terrified of their awe-inspiring powers.

Yet Belthamquar did not concern himself with the girl. Rather he stared upon the eidolon with the shimmering face of Afgorkon. The father of demons was clad in a black cloak, his face was not clearly seen, it was as if a blackness were inside the cloak with the glowing golden sigils etched upon its surface.

"I have not seen this eidolon for five hundred centuries, Afgorkon. Since then, I have assumed it was lost."

"As it was. The woman crouched on the floor, and that big barbarian in the doorway brought it up from what was my necromantic chamber."

The empty blackness turned toward Kothar. Two gleaming red eyes, smoldering with ancient wisdom, studied his big frame. Sweat came out on the Cumberian's face. His animal senses told him he was in the presence of mystery and strange powers. Yet he growled softly, and put his hand on his sword-hilt.

There was a dry chuckle. Belthamquar turned back to the statue. "Who stole the demon light from Eldrak?"

"I do not know. I have tried to find out—and cannot. I know, however, that someone or something is slaying the wizards and sorcerers of Yarth. The dead come from their graves bearing weapons, and where they find the warlocks, there they strike."

Eldrak—who was little more than a pillar of red flame, Kothar thought—said wryly, "Why, if they do that, who will call upon us, offering us sacrifices and rare jewels, plus other things which we enjoy?"

"I have thought of that," murmured Belthamquar.

"And I," breathed the eidolon. "Long have I slept in the worlds I have made, enjoying that which I have created. Yet now it seems I am awake, and aware that I cannot hide away from the call of those who still know life. We must join forces, we three. A necromancer in Yarth is calling upon powers unknown to me, which protects him from my astral eyes.

"If I could search out this protective shield, learn what causes it, I might be able to destroy it and learn the name of him who kills wizards."

"And we shall help," whispered Belthamquar softly.

"Aye, aye," nodded Eldrak. "We shall help!"

The blackness and the glowing redness faded to invisibility. The blurry face on the statue disappeared. Red Lori shivered, still bent before the eidolon, awed and frightened by the terrifying forces her spells had summoned up.

"Red Lori," came the voice.

"Yes, master?"

"Go you with my coffer of scrolls and with this eidolon to the ruins of Radimore in Tharia. Long, long ago Radimore was the focal point of strange powers. It is where this world of Yarth and those nether worlds of Belthamquar, Eldrak, and the other demons once touched, by a happenstance in the time and space continuum. There are our powers best able to be focused.

"And go you soon, if you would live."

Kothar watched the woman shivering. He stepped forward, caught her under an armpit, hoisted her to her feet. She swayed, staring up at him. Her eyes were glassy, she seemed under a terrible emotional stress.

"My body . . . they drew on my body to give the . . . the strength to stay here in this world ... while they talked... I thought they would— kill me with their energies...."

She shuddered, resting her cheek on his chest. Gone was the proud sorceress, she was no more than a fearful woman. And the barbarian found that his feelings toward her were more tender than ever before.

"Where is this Radimore?"

"A few miles south of Phyrmyra, where you found me. It is a desolate place. Legends claim that the gods hate it because of olden blasphemies that happened there, but this I do not believe, after what Belthamquar and Eldrak said. We must go there at once, Kothar."

"After you have eaten," he smiled. "I have no need for food."

"Just the same, you'll eat."

She sought to resist but she was so weak she was like a child as he drew her by an elbow out to the companionway and up the steps to the deck. They went forward to the galley, where Kothar found meat and bread and filled a tankard with nut-brown ale from Aegypton. He feasted with her, and to them came Phordog Fale and Nemidomes, still frightened by what had happened, to listen to Red Lori's account of what had taken place in the cabin.

It was decided that they would land at Zoane, that Flarion would hire horses, and that Kothar would remain on board with the others in case the assassin sent more killing corpses. Red Lori must sleep, the mages decided. She would need all her strength for what was to come.

Flarion offered no argument when the barbarian went to find him. He was oddly pleased, Kothar thought, so much so that he grew suspicious. He put a hand on the young mercenary, gripping his wrist.

"Think not to flee away with Cybala," he rasped. "Those three back there in the gallery could find and destroy you with their arts merely by muttering a few words."

The youth nodded. "I shall not run away. Trust me, Kothar."

The Cumberian did not trust him, there was a triumphant light deep in his eyes that told Kothar he had some plan in mind. "I keep Cybala here. You go alone to Zoane."

"As the two moons pass overhead," nodded the youth.

The ship lay at anchor in the harbor of Zoane. It was just one among many ketches and merchantmen that plied these salt waters carrying oak to Thuum and rich red wine from Makkadonia to Sybaros and the Southlands, herbs, and spices from Ifrokone and Ispahan, weapons from the forges of Abathor, slaves from the Oasian jungles. Zoane was

81

a crossroads of his world, a seaport to rank with Memphor, on the other-sider of the continent. Tar and pitch and the salt winds-blended with the musk smell of the teak-wood ships from below the equator. It was a rich city, Zoane, and here came all the evils and wickednesses of mankind to be sold over counting tables as if they were no more than shawls from Mantaigne.

Flarion found Greyling and five more horses in a stable fronting a cobbled alleyway. The five mounts were big beasts and strong. He bought them, guessing shrewdly that they had been stolen. He paid more than they were worth, but Red Lori had been generous with the golden coins she poured into his purse. On a venture such as this, she assured him, gold and jewels meant nothing.

He was leading his purchases back through the narrow byways and cobbled footpaths when he became aware that he was being followed. He turned, searching the shadows with keen eyes, but he saw nothing more than a dwarf scuttling along close to a building wall. He hailed the midge but the creature never halted. After a time, Flarion walked on with the horses' hooves clip—clopping behind him.

Grovdon Dokk had swum to a quay and found a longboat for hire. He had rowed back to Wave-skimmer and taken off with Kothar and the two mages together with the belly-dancer. Because of the weight of the eidolon, Red Lori had stayed with it on the ship until the captain could return for it.

She was paying Grovdon Dokk off with gold bars when Flarion came up, with the horses. She paused to say, "We'll need a wagon for the statue. Go buy one. Or steal it if you have to."

In minutes he was back with a two-wheeled cart and a harness into which he fitted one of the horses. He helped Cybala into the cart, then gave Kothar a hand swinging the eidolon up onto the floorboards. The cart creaked protestingly, but it took the weight without snapping a wheel.

They headed west toward the meadow-lands beyond Zoane. They could go only as fast as the lorry, so it was at a slow walk that they moved through the city streets. Flarion crowded his horse close to that of Kothar, telling him of the dwarf.

"If he was an informer, we may expect trouble," the barbarian nodded. "Perhaps he saw the gold with which you paid for the horses and ran to tell a thieves' guild. If so, they'll come after us."

But they rode all the night and well into the day without any sign of pursuit. They were deep in the Tharian grasslands, with the hills of western Sybaros a purple line beyond the desert to the north. A wind faintly scented by the high grasses ran here and there, blew about the flocks of birds that dipped and darted, uttering harsh cries.

They camped by a small stream and ate of the food Red Lori had brought from the ship. They slept, with Kothar standing guard.

It was the barbarian who saw the dust cloud far to the east but coming nearer, and it was with a sense of unease that he went to wake Flarion.

"I make it out a body of horsemen, roughly fifty strong" muttered the Cumberian.

Flarion nodded, then, glanced at the big barbarian. "How far is Radimore? Burdened down by the statue, we can't make a good time."

"Then into the cart with Cybala and go as fast as you can. I'll bring up the rear with my horn-bow and hope to slow them down."

Red Lori awoke at a touch, nodded agreement with what the barbarian had done. She stared at the distant dust cloud, then at the little cart trundling off across the plain.

"We can never make it in time. Whatever follows us is coming faster than we can travel."

"Then go ahead, you and the magicians. Use your wizardries to summon up help of some kind." Kothar was at his saddle, lifting his horn from its case. "I'll ride rearguard, keep them back with a few arrows. That ought to give you time to reach the city."

She frowned at him. "You're only sacrificing yourself needlessly. Ride with us, Kothar. We do what we can together or—"

His laughter rang out. "Girl, you've done so much magic-making lately that you forget what, a fighting man can do. Yonder are some rocks, perhaps half a dozen miles away. I'll ride so far with you. And there I stay, to give you others a chance to reach Radimore."

He turned her, pushed her toward the others. "Wake them, get them into their saddles. And if you love life—hurry!"

Chapter Seven

They were mounted within moments and soon galloping after the creaking lorry. To Kothar, bow in hand and his quiver of arrows beside his right leg, life was beginning to make some sense. Not for him the consultations of demons and gods, the whispers of necromancers! This was what he understood, a headlong gallop across the plains with enemies behind him coming fast.

Often he turned in the kak and stared at the oncoming dust cloud. He frowned when he studied it, puzzled and uneasy. That dust cloud could only be made by a large body of men on horseback. But what large body of men would be pelting after them this way? Thieves, yes. But there should be no more than a handful of the sly cut-purses who frequented the streets of Zoane trailing them from the seaport city.

Fifty of the foot-pads banded together to rob half a dozen travelers? It was too incredible to consider. But if their pursuers were not street thugs, what were they? Kothar shook his head as he gripped his horn bow tighter. Well, he would know soon enough.

When they were galloping along the road leading between the rocks, the barbarian drew rein. "Go you on," he shouted to Red Lori, waving a hand. "I stay to hold them up a little while."

She urged her bay mare closer to him, putting out a hand to clasp him. "Be careful, Kothar. Fight your best but—avoid death! Remember," her lips curved into a faint smile, "you belong to me. I don't want anything to happen to you."

Then she was gone after the others, bent above her horse's mane, crouched low in the saddle. Kothar watched her, then swung down from Greyling and began unfastening holding straps. When he was done, he walked in among the rocks carrying the horn-bow and a full quiver.

A leather sack with a little food in it was tossed over a shoulder, balanced by a fat, water-skin. He sniffed at the air, finding it blowing to the eastward, which would give his arrows more speed. His eyes searched among the rocks as he walked.

When he came to a level spot protected by several large boulders that looked almost like shields to his war-wise eyes, he dropped the water-skin and the leather food sack.

Crouching down, he ate slowly, relishing each mouthful. He had an hour at least to wait for that dust cloud to resolve itself into men and horses. Until then he would fill his belly. Dwalka knew when he would get to take another mouthful. He hid Greyling in a little dip.

Then he settled down to wait, his gaze moving out across the grasslands, finding the dust cloud no longer visible because the horses were pounding along on thick grasses now. Faintly he could make out a large number of dots that turned into men on horseback the nearer they came.

He nocked an arrow to his string. His sharp eyes, saw metal helmets and nose pieces and mail shirts under surcoats that bore, the boar design of King Midor. Astonishment held him paralyzed a moment.

Why was King Midor interested in them? It was a question he could not answer. And so, when he found himself faced by an enemy to shoot at, he let go the arrow. It flew fast and straight, burying itself in the chest of a horseman. The rider threw up his arms and pitched sideways from the saddle. Three times Kothar shot. Three men were on the ground bleeding out their lives before the war captain threw up his right arm, realizing they were faced by a sharpshooting foe, and yelled for his men to scatter.

The war captain dropped into the high grasses, holding his small shield chest-high so he could see over its rim. He was a tall man, with a lean middle and a deep chest, with very long arms. His face under the nose-piece and cheek plates of his helmet was swarthy, there was a jagged scar along one side of his jaw. Kothar knew he was a veteran fighting man, known as Captain Oddo of Otrantor.

His men obeyed him implicitly, they were out of their kaks and into the grass within seconds. They made unseen targets now, but Kothar was too impatient to wait until one or another showed himself. He grimaced, not liking what he was about to do, but Red Lori and the others were in bad straits, between the pits of Koforal and the poisonous swamps of Illipat.

He began shooting the horses. Six mounts were down before the war captain bellowed, "They'll leave us afoot if we don't stop them." Evidently he thought that more than one man was doing the bow work. "There can't be many, I only saw two warriors. At them!"

He sprang to his feet, shield up and covering his head and chest as he ran. His men followed him, imitating his posture. Yet Kothar downed three of them despite their quick shield-play. There were too many to stand them all off, and they ran swiftly as men who feared for their lives.

Kothar turned and sped away. They saw him fleeing, but they were convinced that more than one man had been shooting those arrows and so they did not rush after him pellmell and without regard for their own skins. They kept their shields up and their swords ready to stab or slash as they went warily among the rocks.

Kothar ran for the gray horse. Scorning the stirrups he vaulted over its croup and into the Saddle. He kicked Greyling into a gallop.

He rode seemingly recklessly, yet there was no finer horseman anywhere in Yarth than Kothar the barbarian. His strong hand on the reins, his shiftings, in the high-peaked saddle, eased the way of the stallion between the rocks and along those stretches of flat dirt between them.

He made good time, yet always as he rode his eyes searched the tumbled boulders for another spot from which to make a stand. And when he had come to it, he leaped from the saddle, scrambled behind a big boulder, and waited.

The stallion he let wander. Its reins were trailing along the ground, it would not go far. And now Kothar wet a finger, held it up, testing the wind. He grinned coldly. It was still blowing eastward, it would give his shafts a little added distance and power.

He set arrow to bowstring, waiting. The soldiers would discover soon enough that there were no men hidden among the rocks, they would be after him shouting for his blood. Against only one man, they would grow careless for a little while . . . .

The horn bow bent. An arrow sailed high into the sky. It came down fast, so swiftly that no eye saw it until it buried its feathers in the throat of a young warrior. The man tried to Scream, could not, and pitched forward on his face.

The small shields came up, but Kothar was so far away and the arrows moved so swiftly that no man saw them until it was too late. Three more men were down, kicking out their lives, before anyone thought to go back for the horses and ride to meet this archer who shot with such unerring marksmanship.

Then they came between the rocks at a gallop, moving so swiftly that not even Kothar could aim with any hope of success. He flashed one shaft in a man's arm, but wasted four in among the boulders.

He snarled and leaped for his saddle. Greyling ran as he had rarely run before. Out of the rocks he flashed like a silver arrow along the flat savanna. An hour of such racing and Kothar could see, low on the horizon, what had been the city of fabled Radimore, which was perhaps the oldest city on Yarth. Tales were told of Radimore, that it had been the home of those people who first worshiped the dark god, Pulthoom. It was the birthing place of all magicians, for it had been here in the subterranean cellar-ways of this city that magic-first came into being.

He saw. Flarion waiting at the emptiness. which had been the city gate eons ago. The youth raked the seemingly empty savanna with his stare, nodding.

"You came like the wind, faster than the soldiers. Greyling is a horse to be proud of."

"The others?"

"Safe enough, for the nonce. Follow me." They went along the dusty streets until they came to a building set before a city square, its facade covered with grotesque carvings, eroded by wind and rain. Red Lori was there, coming from the building door, with Phordog Fale and Nemidomes, at her elbows. In the background shadows he could make out Cybala, hiding.

"I killed a few, the others follow me," he snapped, dismounting.

Phordog Fale shook his bald head framed in white hair. "I fear it's useless. This is a strange city, very strange. There is an evil about it—"

He broke off, wringing his hands.

Nemidomes wiped his plump, sweating face. "What he means to say is—we're doomed. We perish here, the lot of us."

Kothar looked at the witch-woman. She spread her hands. "He speaks truth. There is a curse of some sort upon it, like a miasma from a poisoned swamp." She shivered, looking about her. "It's in the very air, this evil. It—frightens me."

Kothar tried to cheer her with, "But you three are experts in sorcery!

87

Surely the demons will come to you... protect us...."

"We face more than wizardry," muttered the plump little man. "We deal not with demons but with—things of some other world, another place in the universe. They come and gibber at us, when night-falls As if they were—waiting."

The shadows seemed to lengthen as the barbarian watched. He had fought long, he had ridden across the afternoon to come to Radimore. Now it was dusk, and night was gathering darkness in the sky and in the more shadowy places of the ancient city.

"Let's build a fire," he snarled with the barbarian's directness. "The spirits can't harm us in the light."

Flarion laughed harshly. "Can they not? I think they can. Nevertheless, come with us, Kothar."

He led the way through the deserted, moldy hall of the big building to its back entrance, which gave upon a large courtyard. Here a bonfire blazed, its flames red and leaping. It crackled cheerily, yet Kothar could hear a faint whispering, a breathing, above the snap of fire-devoured twigs.

"They come," moaned Cybala, shrinking close to Flarion.

He saw them first as swirling mists, dancing bits of fog that came from windows and doorways and leaped and twisted in their coming.

They whispered, softly and lightly, laughing shrilly, chuckling in obscene ways. All about them were these gray wisps, sentient and wicked. They edged toward the six travelers in hoppings and skippings that made them the more terrifying by their very lightheartedness.

Kothar yanked out Frostfire and strode to meet them.

Lori screamed, but the barbarian ignored her warning to slash sideways at a twisted bit of mist that slid to envelop him. Through the mist went Frostfire as though it slashed at air. Yet the gray thing touched the barbarian and where it fastened unseen claws, wet and slimy, burned with the fury of a thousand poisoned needles.

The barbarian bellowed, trying to shake-free. They were attacking the others. He saw Red Lori down on the ground, writhing and screaming, trying to battle the thing with her hands. And Phordog Fale was backed against a building wall, pushing, thrusting against a nothingness that ate at him.

Flarion used sword and dagger, but uselessly. In moments he was falling, yet still battling. And Cybala was a step beyond him, hands to her pretty face, screaming. Plump Nemidomes was crouched over a fallen bench, seeking to fend off those stinging mists.

It may have been the magic in the sword Frostfire that hurt the gray mists attacking Kothar. For suddenly as he slashed, their obscene chucklings and merry giggles turned to angry cries and shrill snarls. He could see the gray become scarlet, shot with anger. It seemed also that he could make out a serpentine form within the mists, and something so hideously shaped its very existence was a blasphemy against all that was normal and natural.

He also saw claws sharply pointed, scarlet. Instead of ripping just flesh, they tore into his mail and through the leather of his jerkin. He fought, though he was covered with a hundred wounds. Frostfire moved almost of its own will, in a figure-eight pattern that cut to left and right through those eerie beings.

They slashed the leather of his belt pouch, and out upon the courtyard paving tumbled the jewels and golden coins and bars that he had taken from the tomb of Kandakore. Along the flaggings they bounced while Kothar fought for his very life.

"Afgorkon Aid me! Give me—strength!" he panted.

A serpentinered fog screamed horribly. The claws went away, the beings drew back. Kothar panted, blood running from arms and chest and thighs. His sword was a very heavy weight in his hand, now; he wondered if he could lift it again to defend himself when the things came back.

Yet they did not attack him again. He could hear their hissing speech faintly, as though from far away, as they retreated slowly from him and—from the others. Red Lori was sitting up, a hand to her fallen red hair, looking about her dazedly. Phordog Fale was slumped against the building wall while Cybala knelt weeping over an unconscious Flarion.

Nemidomes picked himself up, stared around wildly. "They're— going! Leaving us. But—Why?"

Kothar shook his head. Lori came to him, touched his bleeding arm and chest. "They cut right through your mail, the leather of your jerkin. Strange. To me their claws were like tiny teeth sunk into my blood, drinking my life. But you—"

The Cumberian shook his sword. "The magic in this thing hurt them, made them angry. They wanted to make me suffer before they took my life.

"Why did they stop, Kothar?"

"I called on Afgorkon."

She shook her head. "No, it was more than that. She drew back, staring at the fallen gems and gold that had come out of his belt-purse. She bent down, ran her fingers across an emerald and a big ruby.

Kothar grinned, "My curse runs true, you see. For possessing Frostfire, I was about to lose more than my life. They took away my treasure first."

The witch-woman shook her head impatiently. "No, no. It was for some other reason, I'm sure. Phordog Fale! Nemidomes! Come help me."

They came running, but it was Lori who cried out, hand darting. Her fingers closed about a disc and lifted it toward the firelight from the campfire. It had grown dark, the city was shrouded by night. Yet, with the leaping flames reflecting on the disc, Kothar could see the intertwinings carved on its surface that had reminded him of a great snake, when he had first seen it, in a Zoane alleyway.

"The disc of Antor Nemillus," breathed the woman.

"I recognize it," the barbarian muttered. Her green eyes glowed up at him. Her breasts moved to her excitement as she said, "Don't you understand? It was this that kept us safe—this!" Her fingers closed around the disc, and triumph flared in her stare. "He gave us—safekeeping with this thing. But those demon beings would only obey—their master!"

Phordog Fale scowled, "But that means—"

"Yes! Antor Nemillus wishes us dead. He sent those—those eerie things to devour us, not knowing who we were, only that we six travelers were dangerous to him. But the servants of Omorphon saw only the disc—Omorphon's self on it. They drew back away from it, thinking us protected by their lord."

She stood up. "We know now Antor Nemillus is the one who has been slaying the magicians of Yarth! He sent soldiers to slay us before we could reach here with the eidolon. When that failed, he summoned up Omorphon's servants and set them upon us. Aye, he knows three of us are magicians, and that we pose a threat to him."

Kothar said, "But he was attacked in Zoane!"

"Someone learned he was the wizard-killer sought to do what we've been trying to do—and failed when you stopped him, Kothar!"

"Find that man, then. Learn what he knows." Red Lori shook her head. "No time for that. Antor Nemillus will know now that we are protected in some manner. He may or may not suspect the cause. We must act fast!"

"But how?" quavered fat Nemidomes. The woman bit her lip, frowning. "Magic won't work," grinned the barbarian. "You've tried that. Even Afgorkon with Belthamquar and Eldrak could not help us. Antor Nemillus is too well protected. Instead—send me."

"You?"

"Make a fake eidolon! Let me carry it to Zoane, offer it to the mage with the assurance that I am a turncoat, that I want no more of you. Let him think I would rather be on his side. Then—I'll take off his head with Frostfire."

She smiled faintly. "The barbarian treatment for any danger—slay it! No, no, we must be clever, Kothar. Clever!"

Yet when they had eaten, speaking all the time of plans and plots, they could not come up with any better idea. Lori did not like the plan, she said as much. Yet she could offer no other solution.

"He will kill you horribly, you know," she told him, "if he suspects the truth."

The Cumberian shrugged, reached for his fur cloak and rolled himself up in it to sleep. The witch-woman brooded at him, sighed, then turned her eyes to the fire to sit there, dreaming

The soldiers of the king came early to Radimore, but they found the barbarian in the gateway with Flarion at his side. Kothar held aloft the safe conduct sigil that Antor Nemillus had given him.

"Why didn't you show that yesterday?" asked Captain Oddo.

"This is the seal of Antor Nemillus. You wear Midor's livery."

The war captain spat, "Same thing, these days. Midor does what his magician says, not having any will of his own. I'm not sure I ought to obey, that device you hold—but I don't dare disobey. We'll ride back to Zoane and get further orders. Then—we may meet again."

He raised his hand, shouted to his horsemen.

They rode back across the savanna in lines of two, like trained veterans. Kothar watched them go, finding a touch of kinship with these cavalrymen inside him. He was a soldier, a mercenary. At another time and in another place he might have been that war captain.

"Damn all magicians," he breathed. Red Lori waited in the courtyard for him. "I have prepared a second eidolon," she muttered, tapping a stone statue that Kothar could not have told from the original. "I have summoned up Afgorkon, asked him to keep his eyes and ears on this simulacra. In such fashion shall we be able to keep in touch with you."

She hesitated, biting her lips. "Don't do something stupid in Zoane. Antor Nemillus is a clever mage, which is why I can't use cantraipal spells to send you to him, you have to go in the cart carrying the eidolon. It would never do for you to arrive in Zoane ahead of those soldiers."

An hour later he was moving through the gate, cartwheels creaking as the horse pulled at its harness straps. Kothar sat on the little seat, Greyling trotted at the end of a tether. His bow and saddle, arrow-quiver and sword lay in the back of the cart beside the statue. It would take several days to reach Zoane at this slow pace; before then, Antor Nemillus might well decide to slay Red Lori and the others.

Three days later he creaked into the seaport city.

The gate guards passed him through. No man or woman sought to stop or even question him as the cart rattled across the cobbles toward the big town mansion which was the property of Antor Nemillus. Only when he came to stand at the oaken door of that house and knock, was there anyone to bar his way.

Then it was merely a servant girl, with long brown hair and an over-tight woolen tunic which showed off her ripe figure, who opened the door to him and stood aside with a flirtatious glance from her dark eyes.

"The master has been expecting you," she murmured.

As he followed her swaying haunches across a flag-stoned lower hall, the barbarian wondered whether the magician knew also of his scheme to slay him. It was in something of a suspicious mood that he came to a stop in a great dining hall where Antor Nemillus sat to breakfast.

The necromancer was in high good humor, waving an expansive hand. "Come join me, man of the Northlands. Sausages, chilled ale, freshly baked bread—ask of me what you will. I remember your face, you see, and the night you saved my life in an alleyway."

Kothar pulled back a chair, perched his rump onto it. Two pretty girls ran to place a wooden platter before him and serving trays heaped with steaming meat within easy reach. The magician watched him with sunken eyes in which the barbarian thought to read a sly mockery.

He ate warily, fearing poison, until the sorcerer taunted him for his fears. "I would never resort to anything so mundane as ground glass or hemlock. No, no. Mine is a better way. If I wanted to be rid of you—I could blast you into the vast abysses where Omorphon dwells. It would not be clean death. No!"

The Cumberian believed him, and so he ate more heartily. When he was done, he spoke of the eidolon, explaining how he fetched it from the sea and how Red Lori spoke to it. Of—how he fought the soldiers and the mist-beings of the serpent-god he told freely and openly, while the mage popped dates into his mouth and munched, nodding his head from time to time.

"It is so my magical waters have showed me, barbarian. All these things you have done, yes. What troubles me is, why should you desert your friends?

"Friends! What friends have I, a sell-sword? Red Lori I put in a silver cage for Queen Elfa of Commoral. Later, I trapped her in the tomb of Kalikalides and sealed it with silver. Lori hates me, she considers me her property."

"And you would be free of her?"

"I like not magic," growled the barbarian, honestly enough, "but I've gotten into something I like no better than I do spells and incantations. I thought that by coming here and giving you this eidolon I stole, I might buy your friendship."

"And you have, Kothar. But I must make test of this statue, you understand that. It may be a cheat, a mere copy. Eh?"

Kothar did not betray himself. "It may. It isn't."

"No, no. But we shall test it, you and I." He rose, his gesture telling the barbarian there was work to be done in his necromantic chambers. Kothar weighed the chances of dragging out his Sword and leaping at the magician.

He decided against it; this apparent friendliness of the wizard smacked too much of a trap. He wasn't even sure this was the real Antor Nemillus before him. Lori had warned him against doing anything stupid. He would wait, biding his time.

He followed the mage upward along a narrow stone staircase to an upper floor. There was a great apartment here, walled with stone and with a high, vaulted ceiling from which, hung many cages at the end of chains. In the cages were bats and toads, black cats and newts, together with other small animals from which Antor Nemillus was wont to draw the things he needed for his incantations. Long counters were laden with crucibles and alembics, while the walls contained various magical instruments.

In the center of the flagstones which formed the floor, a red pentagram was shaped of crimson stone, before which was placed a prie-dieu on which rested a massive volume bound in leather, thrown open at a certain conjuration. The false eidolon had been set up behind this lectern.

Antor Nemillus invited Kothar to step into the pentagram with him, with a wave of the hand and a friendly smile. "Let me demonstrate my magicks, barbarian—so that you will know you have made the right choice in coming to me."

The Cumberian shifted his sword closer to his hand. The false eidolon would not work. How could it? Antor Nemillus would know he had been betrayed. Therefore, so that the magician killer might not destroy him with some magical spell, he would run cold steel into his flesh as soon as he made the discovery.

He stepped inside the pentagram, followed by the mage.

Antor Nemillus put his hands on the open book, began reciting from its pages in a deep voice. As those words washed, across the vast chamber, Kothar reached for his dagger-hilt. His iron fingers locked

94

around its braided haft.

He held the dagger ready, but could not use it.

For this incantation which the magician-killer was using turned the blood in a man's veins to ice. He stood there motionless, unable to do more than see and hear. Though he strained, his muscles were locked in a paralytic spasm. And the necromancer went on reciting. The far wall of the chamber turned to fog, drifted away, opening a cantraipal door into those nether spaces where swung the worlds of Belthamquar and Eldrak, Gargantos and Dakkag.

And—the world of—

Omorphon!

Swiftly went the chamber across those abysses. Sweat stood out on the barbarian's forehead as his body swayed to the tricks of his eyes. The pentagram was, the only floor beneath his war-boots. It swept at terrifying speed above those black gulfs of emptiness, racing always onward toward—

A glowing, up ahead. A whiteness that seemed to crawl as might a maggot across the dark deeps of space! And in that whiteness— something that twisted and turned, writhed and wriggled. Even Kothar did not need to ask what it was. Or who was turning its flattened head toward the moving pentagram.

Wicked eyes in a serpent head, wise with the knowledge of the ages evil, stared at the on comers. Larger grew Omorphon. Larger, larger, until it filled the universe about them and the pentagram with its two human riders was no more than a midge before those beady eyes.

"I see you, mage. My servants complain that you gave their victims the disc with my symbol on it, as a protection against their—hungers."

"I did, dread Omorphon. Before I knew they were to be victims. These six whom I intended to feed to your servitors are nothing to me. They shall be fed to your fiends yet. I have sent soldiers to fetch them from Radimore."

"It is well. But why come to me now?"

"There is an eidolon in my chambers. I suspect it is not the true eidolon of the mage Afgorkon who lived fifty thousand years ago———"

"And still lives, Antor Nemillus, in his own Worlds."

"Ah, does he so? Then perhaps the eidolon is not so false as I imagined."

"There is a way to test it. Long ago Afgorkon and I were—good friends. The spell of stone tongues will make it speak, if it be that true eidolon."

"My gratitude, great Omorphon. And to show my good will, send your servitors to my chambers, where they shall find their feast awaiting them."

The serpent god inclined its head.

Instantly the pentagram was moving back across those vast infinitudes of space. There was no wind, no sensation of flying other than the fact that the stars moved slowly to left and right of them. Those tiny blue points of light came and receded, and Kothar felt that they were traversing unfathomable stretches of mega-cosmic emptiness.

The pentagram firmed.

The stood in the chamber of Antor Nemillus once more. And across the great-room-grouped together, and unmoving as himself—the Cumberian saw Red Lori; with plump Nemidomes and old Phordog Fale flanking her. Flarion and Cybala stood to one side, the belly-dancer half fainting in her terror.

There was fear on all their faces, even on the lovely features of the witch-woman. Possibly her green eyes showed more horror than the others, for she knew what was to be their fate, she understood that Omorphon the serpent deity had aligned itself with the mage of Zoane in his quest for supremacy, on Yarth.

To die by Omorphon's servitors was not a nice death.

"Kothar!" she whimpered. "Aid us!" Antor Nemillus turned, smiled at the barbarian. "Tell them, Kothar. Tell them how you stole the eidolon of Afgorkon and brought it here to me."

"I did as he says," muttered the Cumberian. "And now to test that statue," nodded the mage.

With long, pallid fingers he turned the pages of the book until he came at last to the spell of stone tongues. And he recited what was written there, faintly smiling when he heard Red Lori moan in her anguish, and saw Nemidomes wipe at the sweat running down his face.

The eidolon was silent.

"What?" cried Antor Nemillus in pretended dismay. "Does not this spell work? Omorphon himself said I should attempt it, and that if the eidolon spoke with me, it would prove to be that fabled simulacra of dread Afgorkon."

"So speak, statue-speak!"

The magician waited, shaking his head dolefully. "It seems it is no more than ordinary stone, perhaps it was even conjured into being by Red Lori who has appointed herself my nemesis. Is it so, redhead?"

Red Lori was silent.

"Too bad, too bad. In such case, I must blast it, then summon the servants of the serpent god to—feast."

Cybala shrieked, head thrown back and quivering.

Antor Nemillus laughed, lips twisted in a cruel smile. "The dancer is blameless, I feel, yet Omorphon would not like it if I withheld her from their eating."

The belly-dancer moaned and sagged against Flarion, who held her in his arms. The youth was white with the abysmal terror that held him in its grip; like Kothar, he could fight anything animal or human, but he knew a primal fear where demons of the nether spaces were concerned.

And yet, he drew his sword.

Kothar felt a faint throbbing coming to his war-boots from the pentagram. He was puzzled by it. It sounded like the beating of a giant heart, but where in Zoane would such a heart exist? Throb, throb, throb! It made a steady cadence throughout the town house.

Antor Nemillus did not hear it, apparently. Or if he did, he was so familiar with it that he paid it no attention. Instead he turned and Smiled coldly at the Cumberian.

"Did you know this eidolon was false, barbarian? Are you part of the plot against me, whereby Red Lori would pull me down to death and make empty vaporings of all my dreams? I could use a man like you, but not if you are one of these conspirators. So I abjure thee.

Speak!"

Kothar fought the magic that flooded his great body, fought and groaned against the telling, but the magic of Antor Nemillus was stronger than his muscles. His lips writhed back and his tongue curled to life.

"The eidolon is—false! It was made by the witch-woman and given to me to bring to you, that you might betray yourself so we would know you for the magician-killer. It succeeded of its purpose but—"

"But the knowledge will do you no good! For I have condemned you all to Omorphon, who will feast on your energies through his servitors. See! . . They come!"

The mage swept his black-robed arm in an arc.

The walls faded. Leaping across the void, sweeping with dizzying speed toward their world, were the eerie beings whom Kothar had battled in Radimore. He saw their curving gray shapes, their fog-like fiendishness, and knew they were all doomed.

He groaned. Underfoot the throbbing was becoming louder, more menacing, and he wondered if these were the sounds made by those oncoming mist beings. He strove against the spell that held him in thrall, fighting vainly to free Frostfire so that he might go down fighting, at least.

Nemidomes was a whimpering mass of wet flesh pressed against a stone wall. Phordog Fale was rigid, eyes wide as if he already looked on that land which is said to exist after death. Red Lori was biting her knuckles, and Flarion stood over the crumpled form of the unconscious Cybala.

They were like hogs to the slaughter. Antor Nemillus threw back his head and laughed. His laughter only echoed the swirlings of the serpentine things through the vanished chamber wall and onto the flagstones. Cybala awoke, screamed.

And at that moment, thunder shook the house.

Chapter Eight

So terrific was that awesome burst of sound that Antor Nemillus looked upward; even the gray life-drinkers paused. A brick fell from the vaulted ceilings, missing the barbarian by a foot. The thunderclap shattered their eardrums a second time, and now the building swayed. Antor Nemillus cursed in his pentagram and sprang toward his open grimoire.

The stone wall quivered, stones fell.

A great hand—a thing of stone and rock, hideously carved and with strange spells and incantations limned on its rock surface—reached in the opening it had made, and stabbed forward. Blunt fingers closed around the squirming, screaming necromancer.

"Dread Omorphon! Awful being of the nether hells—aid me!"

Antor Nemillus tried to fight it, but his hands could do nothing against the solid rock out of which that other hand was formed. The fingers tightened, and now the magician began to swell curiously at chest and legs, as if other parts of his body were being forced into them by that frightful grip. His face became purple with congested blood. His eyes bulged hideously, a trickle of blood ran from his open mouth.

The magician tried to cry out, could not.

Another hand came into the chamber, making its own opening by crashing through another part of the wall. It slapped at the whirling gray fog-things, smashing two of them flat, and as it did, tiny scarlet bubbles burst and splattered a malodorous ichor across the flagstones. The other serpentine beings squealed, shrieked, turned to flee.

The stone hand was lightning, darting as might a human hand after flies, catching up those things and squeezing them until they plopped and died, gushing that noisome fluid, Only two got away, darting back into the spaces vaguely glimpsed behind the stone wall. The others lay in tiny puddles of their own slime, lifeless.

Antor Nemillus finally burst. His chest and legs—or what had been these portions of his body—were so filled with that which had been in his middle that the skin of his torso and his thighs exploded. Bits of blood and flesh flew here and there.

The stone hand holding his body opened its fingers. The dead magician dropped to the flaggings, lay inert, And the spell on Kothar went away.

The big Cumberian shook himself, leaped from the pentagram to catch Red Lori the witch-woman as she swayed oddly, overcome by the reaction to her terror. She sagged against him, let him lift her up and hold her close.

"You did what you planned to do," he growled.

"But not—this way," she breathed.

She stared at the huge stone hands, gruesomely stained and soiled, as they withdrew out of the openings in the walls through which they had come. Behind them, Flarion was lifting Cybala from the floor. Phordog Fale was pushing away from the wall where he had been so close to fainting. Nemidomes was still sobbing fitfully, the aftermath of his fright making him shiver like pale jelly.

"Are we truly—saved?" whimpered Cybala. "If the gods so will," growled Flarion. Kothar carried Red Lori, whose legs were so shaky she did not trust her weight to them, across the room toward a narrow window. They stared out at the city of Zoane in the fading sunlight of a late afternoon, seeing its streets clogged with men and women staring upward, silent before the awe that held them.

"Look," whispered the witch-woman.

The barbarian saw a stone statue—the eidolon of Afgorkon—grown to an immense height. Its shadow, cast by the setting sun, appeared to dance across the rooftops of the city. It towered high, titanic, an incredible monster from the worlds of magic. Blood and ichor dripped from its stone fingers. It had no face. This was its awfulness, its cantraipal horror.

It turned on a heel and walked away to the west. Toward ancient Radimore, Kothar thought. Its stone feet made muted thumpings on the ground, that came upward to the flagstone floor of this town house chamber; it had been these he had felt as he stood within the pentagram with Antor Nemillus.

"We must follow," breathed Red Lori.

"But why? Your task is done."

She stirred against him. "Have you forgotten the sacrifice? He must be offered a living maiden. Otherwise, he may choose to stay within our world—like that."

"Florian won't like it," Kothar growled.

The witch-woman smiled cruelly. "It doesn't matter what he likes. Or the girl, either. Their destiny is linked with mine, they must, obey."

She stirred against him. "Have you forgotten?" She paused, then called, "Phordog Fale! Nemidomes!"

The magicians came hurrying across the floor to her. They seemed to have recovered a bit of their normal color, and something of their old bravery.

"We must return to Radimore at once," the woman told them. "We have one last task to perform. Flarion! Cybala! Come you with us."

They went down the stone steps away from the shattered chamber and out onto the cobbles of the courtyard, where there were horses waiting. Kothar swung Red Lori into the high-peaked saddle of her bay mare, then mounted up on Greyling. At a canter, he led the way into the crowded streets of the city. And as he did so, he urged the gray warhorse nearer the mare.

"Stay you close to my stirrup, Lori," he muttered.

The men and women of Zoane were in holiday mood, as if some enormous weight had been lifted from their shoulders. They were drunk, reeling about with wine-skins in their hands, their garments half torn from their bodies. An air of Saturnalia was everywhere, a forgetfulness of daily living, a need for merrymaking.

"They may prove dangerous, they may seek to drag us from our saddles to join their revels. I'll break a few heads, if need be, to get us through."

The people ignored them, they were too concerned with their drinking and their wenching to bother about six strangers. Toward nightfall, their mood might turn ugly. The barbarian knew it was the way of drinkers at feasting time. He touched the gray warhorse with a toe, urged it to a faster canter.

He could hear words occasionally from the mob.

"———gone, we can live again!"

"Aye, no need to fear the taking of our wives and daughters for the use of Antor Nemillus and the king!"

"It might be a good thing if Midor died, as Well!"

"To the palace, then. Kill the old goat." They came to a few streets where town houses stood fence by railing with one another, away from the throngs and the merrymakers. It was quiet here, Kothar sensed a frightened face or two peering out from behind draperies and shutters. From here he could see a little park ahead, and beyond that the start of the caravan road to distant Romm and Memphor.

Once on that highway, they would make good time.

All that night they went at a gallop along the hard-packed dirt of the trade road, until they were well within the boundaries of Tharia. Then Kothar turned from that highway eastward toward Radimore.

They came into the ancient ruins at midday, weary with long riding. Red Lori swayed oddly in her saddle; she was near her limits of endurance, the big barbarian realized. He leaped from the saddle, caught her as she lifted a leg over the kak, lowered her to the ground.

"I'm weary. Weary," she murmured. "Then sleep," he nodded.

He caught her up in his massively muscled arms, walked with her to the inner court where he had fought the mist-beings of Omorphon, and laid her down upon the pile of soft grasses that had been her pallet.

"I will make sacrifice later, Kothar," she murmured, smiling and letting him drape her in his fur cloak.

He waited until she was sleeping before he turned and went in search of Flarion. He found the youth with his arms about Cybala in a darkened corner of the quadrangle, whispering to her.

"Mount and ride," he told him. "Travel toward Ebboxor, where I will meet you—when I can."

Cybala pushed her black hair back from her eyes. "Does danger threaten us here?"

"It threatens you, girl. Red Lori plans to offer you to Afgorkon as a sacrifice."

The belly-dancer gasped, shrank closer to Flarion. "Is this why she chose me to accompany you? That she might slay me—when Afgorkon did her will?"

"Mount and ride, stop asking silly questions!" Flarion smiled faintly, "We travel at once. And, Kothar—my thanks!"

They ran lightly toward their horses. Their mounts were weary with the long night galloping, but Flarion would walk them, with the girl beside him, until fresh strength came back into their legs. Then he would mount and gallop toward Ebboxor to the north. It was imperative they leave Radimore, be far away when Red Lori awoke.

Kothar turned toward Phordog Fale and Nemidomes where the two magicians sat crouched about a little fire the plump man had made.

"Go you also away from here," he growled. Nemidomes protested, "My backside is sore, and my legs are jelly. I shall wait and eat, and decide with the witch-woman what we shall do."

Kothar grinned coldly. "The witch-woman is about to sacrifice a girl who won't be here," he rasped, waving a hand after Cybala and Flarion who moving down the cobbled street toward the broken gate. "What do you think Afgorkon will do, being deprived of his sacrifice?"

Phordog Fale frowned worriedly. "It's a thought to worry one," he admitted. "I for one, would not choose to stay and face Afgorkon's wrath—having seen what his eidolon did to Antor Nemillus."

"Nor I," the plump mage murmured.

They rose to their feet and walked toward their horses, with the big barbarian treading on their heels. The morning sun was high—it was almost midday—and a soft breeze was blowing through the dead city.

"Why not use a magic spell to leave?" wondered Kothar.

Phordog Fale turned and stared at the barbarian, nodding. "Aye, a spell. I have been so busy riding horseback lately, I've forgotten I'm a necromancer."

Nemidomes beamed his delight, "Ah, to be back in Vandacia once again, not forced out of fear to hide in that charnel house. I owe you much, Kothar!"

"And I," nodded Phordog Fale The shook hands solemnly.

Nemidomes wrapped himself in his cloak, closed his eyes and whispered a word. His outline shimmered. Kothar could see the stone wall behind that mistiness for an instant, then the plump man was gone.

Phordog Fale snorted, "A clumsy spell, that one. It does not drain the body energies, true. Yet it is slow, Too slow for me. Observe!"

The tall, lean man chanted words in a language unknown to Kothar. Instantly, he was gone. The Cumberian grinned, shaking his head. "I would rather know that little song than the word Nemidomes used, he thought, if I had to leave a place in a hurry." He laughed and moved toward Red Lori.

It was warm in this midday, and there was an ache in his body, now that the need for action was at an end. He sank down beside the witch-woman and closed his eyelids. Almost at the same moment, he fell asleep.

A hand on his arm shook him awake to the sight of stars in the sky. The lovely face of his companion was bent above him. "Where are the others? Cybala? Where has she gone?"

"I sent her away with Flarion. Go back to sleep."

He heard a gasp, felt fingernails sink into his bare forearm. "Wake up, you! You—thing! I promised her life to Afgorkon. You knew that!"

"Afgorkon takes no sacrifices."

"He does. He will. Oh, get up!" The barbarian rose to his feet. The city ruins were silent, lost and lovely, having forgotten the lives they sheltered once, long ago. The starlight was weak and pale, but Kothar could make out the eidolon standing where he had left it when he had taken its simulacra to Zoane. His eyes pierced its stone hands, folded now against its sides. Those rock fingers were stained and befouled with the blood of Antor Nemillus and with the ichor squashed from the servitors of dread Omorphon.

"What are you going to do with it?" Red Lori stared from the barbarian to the eidolon. "I must summon its spirit, as I promised. But—without Cybala to offer it...."

She drew closer to the Cumberian. Kothar scowled, staring at the image. Was he mistaken, was it a trick of the light—or had the statue moved? No, by Dwalka! It was moving, turning its rock head toward them.

"Aye, Red Lori. I am here. Where is this life you offered me?"

The eidolon grew a little. It was not the titanic monster that had slain Antor Nemillus, it rose upward only until it was the height of a tall man. Yet now it turned more fully toward the barbarian and the witch-woman, and though it had no face, the Cumberian sensed the awful life imprisoned in that thing of rock.

"I wait, Red Lori. Where is the sacrifice?" She swallowed twice before she could reply. "I have—none! The girl fled away with Flarion."

A chuckle was its answer. "I saw the barbarian send them away. I have no quarrel with him for his action. Yet where shall I find my payment?"

The girl beside Kothar shuddered. A whiteness came to her cheeks, and her eyes seemed to grow as she stared at the eidolon.

"I know—not, Afgorkon."

"Then I shall take other life in its place. Your life, witch-woman!" The eidolon stirred, turned and moved toward Red Lori.

"By Dwalka—no!" roared Kothar.

His arm tightened about the girl, thrust her behind him. His hand he put on the hilt of Frostfire, half drawing it from—the scabbard. Red Lori was shaking fitfully, convulsed with terror.

"What would you, Kothar?" asked the statue.

"Her—life?"

"And what price have you, a pauper, to offer me in exchange for that life? You own—nothing. It was not your doing, this summoning up of my spirit from where I lay in the fifty worlds of my own creation! I have no argument with you, so—step aside."

Kothar drew his sword. His eyes ran down the blued steel blade, slid over the golden crosspiece, the braided hilt, the red jewel affixed to its pommel. He sighed softly. There was a sorrow in him, a wretchedness of spirit, yet he did not hesitate.

"Take—back—Frostfire," he growled. He flung the blade across the courtyard so that it clanged on the cobblestones before the eidolon. It lay there, mute and beautiful, gathering sunbeams along its blade.

There was a silence. "You would give up Frostfire?" His mouth was dry, his tongue stuck to the roof of his mouth, but the barbarian nodded. When he could speak, he almost snarled.

"Aye—I would Let Red Lori be. Take the Sword."

The witch-woman gasped beside him, she pressed closer as if to assure him that by choosing her, he chose well. His nostrils caught the scent of her perfume, his flesh knew the smoothness of her own where her arm brushed his side. She was still afraid, he sensed from the hurried rise and fall of her breasts, but she was so curious as to what Afgorkon would do, she no longer quivered.

The faceless thing considered them as they stood side by side with the barbarian's heavily muscled arm about Red Lori's slim body. The sun beat down, and somewhere in the ruins a bird chattered. Otherwise, there was only the brooding silence.

Then: "Take up Frostfire, barbarian! It is too lovely a thing to lie hidden in my death chamber. And besides, it comes to me that you will make good use of it in the days and years to come.

"No, I seek not Frostfire. Nor the life of the redheaded wench you seem to love. Yet there is something I must do to her.

"Red Lori—come you forward!"

The woman stirred within the clasp of Kothar's arm. He caught the moan of fear in her throat. He would have moved to thrust himself between her and the eidolon except that his own body seemed turned to the same stone as that from which the statue had been carved. His arm fell away as the redhead moved forward.

His eyes watched her walk slowly, gracefully, toward the statue. In her Mongrol garb, she seemed only a pretty girl. The blouse was torn, shredded from long usage, so he could see the pale skin of her back. Under the leather kilt, her legs were curving columns. He wanted to reach out, catch and hold her.

The statue waited as she neared it. Then lifted its stone arms and put its hands on Red Lori's shoulders, gripping her gently. Where those stone fingers touch, a faint miasma rose upward like steam. The girl shook, but made no sound.

The stone hands lowered.

Red Lori crumpled and lay on the courtyard cobblestones. Over her motionless body, the eidolon stared at the barbarian. It spoke no word but turned and clumped away, its stone feet making those same thumping sounds. Kothar watched it move between the shattered columns of an ancient temple and disappear from view.

He stirred, his chest lifted as he sucked in air. He ran to the girl, turned her over, sliding an arm beneath her pale neck. Her eyes were closed, but she breathed-red lips slightly parted, breasts lifting and falling. Kothar bent his head, pressed lips to that soft mouth.

She stirred, opened her eyes. Those green eyes saw him, but they knew him not. Her eyes went back and forth around the courtyard buildings.

"Where—where am I?" she whispered, shrinking slightly from his arm. "Who am I? And—who are you?"

Kothar sighed. Afgorkon had taken his sacrifice, after all. He had robbed Red Lori of her necromantic knowledge, even of her memory. She was indeed, little more than a lovely, shepherdess or milkmaid now. The barbarian grinned. This was the way he had always wanted her.

"You belong to me," he told her. "I—bought you in a slave market in Zoane."

She frowned at him prettily. "I don't remember."

"You had an—accident. But never mind that. Your name is Lori and you belong to me. So come, wench—stir yourself. We've a long ride ahead of us."

His big hand helped her to her feet. She pushed her red hair from her face, she stared down at herself, at her worn, travel-stained garments. Her cheeks flushed faintly when she saw how much of her body was revealed through the tears and rips.

"Fetch the food bags," he said gently. They rode together out of Radimore just as the sun was going down in the west. They had not far to go, they would be in Ebboxor before midnight. And from Ebboxor? Where would he turn Greyling after that? He was tired of spells and incantations and magicians. There was a yearning for something more substantial than necromancy in his heart.

He rode thoughtfully beside the silent girl. When they came to Ebboxor, there was a red fire blazing and Flarion sitting beside Cybala, who leaned against his encircling arm. They would have risen, but Kothar waved them aside. He helped Red Lori down, watched as she took out meat and bread from the saddlebags.

"What ails her?" wondered Flarion, studying the girl.

"Afgorkon took away her memory." They ate, and when they were done, Kothar drew the girl down beside him on his fur cloak. He made her pillow her red head on his chest, so he could put an arm about her and hold her close.

"Who am I? What was my past life?" she whispered.

"Later, girl. Sleep now."

They slept as once before they had slept amid these ruins. And with the coming of morning, as once before, the barbarian woke with a sword-point at his bare throat. He stared up at a hard bronzed face along the jaw of which ran a jagged scar. The steel camail made tinkling sounds as the war captain lowered his head slightly.

"We meet once more, barbarian. This time, you have no bow in hand, you have no weapons of any kind."

The soldiers with Captain Oddo were few in number. There were only six that he saw, until a seventh came from between two stone pillars carrying half a dozen water-skins. One he handed to Oddo of Ottrantor, the others he passed among the six hard-bitten men who rode behind the war captain.

Flarion was on the ground beside Cybala, both of them trussed like fowls for the bake ovens. Red Lori was also tied at wrists and ankles, and she stared at him dumbly, like patient beast waiting for its master to save her.

Oddo grinned coldly. "You did me a lot of harm, barbarian. Not only on the road to Radimore, but in Zoane as well." He lifted the water-skin, putting the narrow nozzle between his lips and quaffing deep.

The back of his worm velvet sleeve worked across his lips. "We came so fast from Zoane, we had no time to fill our water-skins. It was a long, dusty ride."

Kothar growled, "What harm did I do you in Zoane?"

"Pah! You helped destroy Antor Nemillus, who was my master. Not Midor, no. That fat slug took orders from his mage. I wore his livery, but I was the mage's man. Well, now—that's all ended, thanks to you. So you shall pay."

His eyes ran up and down Red Lori. "I'll take her as part payment of

108

the debt you owe me. The other one," his head jerked at Cybala, "my men can have. You die, barbarian—to pay the rest of the debt."

Captain Oddo grimaced putting a hand to his middle. "Father of demons—what foul poison was in that water? It eats in my belly like a snake!"

Kothar glanced beyond the war captain at the Seven soldiers. They too, were making contorted faces, their hands clawing at their bellies. Captain Oddo took a step, shuddering.

"You men—come here!" he bawled. His men were in no position to obey. Three of them were on their knees, the others were staggering about and moaning. The barbarian waited, watching Oddo of Ottrantor, who was trying to lift his sword and strike at him. Almost gently, the Cumberian withdrew the sword from those nerveless fingers.

"The curse of Ebboxor, Oddo," he muttered. The war captain fell to sprawl out on the ground. Kothar stood above him, asking, "Saw you not the skeletons as you rode into camp? No, I suppose not. It makes no difference, now. I think Afgorkon may have put an added thirst in your throats as you rode this way, however."

He waited with the animal patience of the barbarian until Captain Oddo and his men were dead. Then he cut Lori free, and from her he went to Flarion and Cybala. When they stood beside him, he nodded his head.

"It is over, all of it. Lori and I ride west toward the lands of the robber barons. I am weary of sorcery and wizards. I would take employment with the thieves, perhaps even get to command a band of my own. It is in my mind that a smart man might unite those warring baronies and make a kingdom for himself."

"What of her?" wondered Flarion, gesturing at the redheaded woman who stood rubbing her wrists where the ropes had bitten.

"She has no memory. I'll tell her only what I think she ought to know. Then may-hap I'll marry her. Who knows?"

He walked toward the girl who smiled at him, weakly but with promise. Her green eyes met his and fell before his stare. Flarion turned and strode toward Cybala. He and the belly-dancer would head north into Makkadonia beyond Sybaros. Idly he swung his head and looked behind him.

Kothar was lifting the smiling girl into the kak.

END

Thank you for purchasing Gardner Francis Fox's Sword & Sorcery classic: Kothar and the Wizard Slayer.

Find out more about Mr. Fox by visiting

GARDNERFFOX.com

Made in the USA
Middletown, DE
31 October 2019

77754531R00066